Ash Dogs

Ash Dogs
A Novel by Justin Nicholes

Cover art by Mike McGovern

Another Sky Press
Portland, Oregon

This is a first edition perfect bound published 2008
Printed in the United States of America
ISBN 0-9776051-6-7

Text copyright Justin Nicholes
Contact Justin at justin@anothersky.org

Cover artwork copyright Mike McGovern
Contact Mike at www.mempdx77.com

Cover Design by Ryan Scott
Mexican Sun God Logo by Ryan Scott
Contact Ryan at www.ryanscottdesigns.com

Interior design by Kristopher Young

Another Sky Press logo by Steven Spikoski
Contact Steven at www.stevenspikoski.com

Plato translation by W.H.D. Rouse
Great Dialogues of Plato, Mentor, 1956

Ash Dogs brought to you by
Another Sky Press
P.O. Box 14241
Portland, Oregon 97293
www.anothersky.org

Dear Reader,

Another Sky Press is a non-traditional publishing company located in Portland, Oregon. We operate under a progressive publishing and distribution paradigm that aims to directly benefit both audience and author.

The entire text of this novel is available for free online with a contribution requested but not required. We believe you, the reader, should be able to decide the value of art.

You may also purchase a trade paperback of this novel directly from our website at a sliding scale price that you set: the fixed third-party printing and shipping costs plus an optional contribution. This allows you to decide how much the author and publishing team earn by contributing at a level that is comfortable to you both ethically and financially. Removing middlemen such as bookstores and distributors (which can account for over half the cover price) allows us to ensure that significantly more money actually goes to the author.

If you came across your copy of this book via a library, used bookstore or friend please consider contributing directly to the author at our website. This promotes passing along a book when you're finished with it (thus saving trees) while still allowing each reader to compensate the author if they choose.

Embrace the future. Support that which you love.

Thank you,

Another Sky Press

www.anothersky.org

psst! pass it on. ♺

For my brother,
Bradley Ryan Nicholes,
the truest artist I've ever known.

BOOK 1

GRIEVANCE

Here is no water but only rock
T.S. Eliot, 'The Waste Land'

CHAPTER 1

Marcus's platoon of thirty-nine guarded a gas station in the Al-Salaam district of Baghdad. It was 109 degrees. A wall in front of him fenced off city blocks, and the ground beyond spread level, so only smoke plumes or palm crowns peeked through coils of razor wire. Behind Marcus rippled waves of sand over acres of arid earth.

Exhaust burned his nostrils and numbed his tongue. The automobiles snaked back in a line for more than a mile and blared their horns. When the cars, trucks, and vans neared the gas station bay (engines quaking the ground he guarded), the line split into four prongs, each approaching a pump thruway. Shoving matches or brawls broke out where vying drivers branched or walls funneled traffic onto the service road.

Marcus gripped his M-16 in a two-handed ready carry and chomped a saltine. Hot sugary air wafted off automobile radiators. He watched the back of his buddy Leroy, who profiled drivers. Leroy had the slow, stocky frame of a fullback, and his M-16's muzzle bore a bayonet. With it, he stabbed black-market jerry cans hidden in trunks. Vendors lugged uncut cans along the line of automobiles and cried, charging five times gas station price. A visor shaded Leroy's eyes, so the sun scorched only his cheeks and chin to a coppery black.

Leroy rapped on the driver's side window of a van. At the same time, Marcus inhaled a jagged corner of the saltine. He gripped his throat. He was choking but didn't want Leroy to see. He was supposed to have Leroy's back. *That's how niggas get ran up on,* Leroy would holler. Marcus's vision blurred as he bent forward to hack it out. The M-16 dangled at his knees. He went blind and lurched to the ground and at last coughed the saltine loose. Crouching, he caught his breath. *I know, I know,* he thought. He stood up, and the earth and sky wobbled.

That morning in the platoon's makeshift weightroom, in front of Leroy, Marcus had almost shown he was no longer a committed marine. *Honor, courage, commitment,* Marcus had thought, recalling the tripartite Warrior Code drill

3

sergeants had lectured about in bootcamp, and suddenly his arms had buckled under the weight of the bar. He relinquished the two-hundred pounds to Leroy and sat up. "What you groaning for?" Leroy said, and Marcus stood, blood pulsing through his head. "Wasn't groaning," Marcus said. His vision blurred, and he found himself grinding his teeth. Leroy, then, must've known Marcus was remembering the woman. Leroy muttered and plopped down on the weight bench. Dead skin dusted his sable body so that, in spite of his bullish frame, Leroy looked ghostly. The sun burned Marcus's scalp through the barred window, and Leroy, looking up into Marcus's eyes, only half-ironically rapped out the three core values they'd sworn to during recruit training. Marcus clasped his mouth, scowled profoundly, then leapt forward to smack his fist into Leroy's shoulder. Leroy recoiled and mumbled about how critically he could hurt Marcus, but finally he spit in the sand, and after Marcus added ninety pounds to the bar, Leroy leaned back to finish his morning reps. He groaned pushing the weight, and Marcus watched his spit evaporate.

Now it was noon, and Leroy, the lone sentry, demanded the driver of the van get out. The driver clutched the steering wheel. Finally Leroy yanked the van door open and argued with the driver in Arabic. He wanted the man to unlock the back doors. Marcus trotted towards them. The man wrenched around in the driver's seat and snatched something from beside him. He cradled a bundle to his chest and slid out, and Leroy stumbled back, his mouth shaped into an O.

Marcus ran forward, knowing Leroy would've pulled off a headshot if the man had been a bomb risk, while people all around the van shuffled away. The man was wasp-waisted and wore a vanilla gown stained around the knees. His face burnt violet, and a bird's-nest beard brushed over the bundle in his arms. He was trying to show something to Leroy, presented the bundle as though it were a book too stout to hold in his outstretched arms. Leroy shuffled backwards and aimed the bayonet-tipped rifle. As Marcus closed in, he realized what the man was holding. It was an infant, and something was wrong with its eyes.

4

Two months later, Marcus gripped the hospital blanket in fists. His bones ached from lying still. The bed sheets clung to him, and blood, soaking through the bandage on his hip, stained the sheet. Leroy was wheezing in the next bed. Wire threaded down the middle of his skull. Before, Leroy had swelled with muscle, and when he'd move, flesh shifted like tectonic plates on his shoulders, arms, and thighs. In the medical center, Leroy's body had lost all form. His torn up skin resembled tilled earth. *Marcus, control yourself,* he thought, but the woman in the street gasped for air, and the next day, on another street, the man in the vanilla gown detonated the bomb taped to his chest.

The platoon had been ordered to hunt down protesters who'd lobbed cocktail bombs over the security wall at automobiles lined up for fuel, and Marcus and Leroy braced themselves spreading fields of fire, and that's when one of Marcus's three-round bursts must've struck the black-robed woman's abdomen. Now that woman swirled in currents above Marcus's bed. The currents resembled ashes flying from fire or a congregation of moths. With her, other shapes formed.

A white-breasted plover fluttered in the void. The sight returned Marcus to the age of thirteen and to the Orwell baseball field where that bird, over spring, had built a nest in a rut in left-center field. At practice one early afternoon, Marcus had tried to drive the long-legged plover off the field for its own good. He'd thrown a rock towards it sidearm, and the reckless toss struck the nest. Yolk arched behind the plover's bowed legs and hung motionless in Marcus's memory before the bird inspected the mess, took flight, and circled him. The bird cried, and everyone, Marcus's friends, the middle-aged coach, gawked in horror and inched away as though they'd witnessed a murder.

In the hospital, his cheek twitched, so he brushed his fingertips over the burned skin. The explosion had scorched half his face. The burned half was raw-pink and pockmarked while the unburned side was the same old cocoa brown. According to the surgeon, a splinter of finger bone had pierced his left leg, damaged the iliotibial band, and, like a tick, burrowed itself halfway into the femoral head.

The fifth floor room's window was behind him, but Nurse Sheila drew the blinds at night. During cooler days, she cracked the window open, muttering at the pollution. Tires swished over the freeway, and car doors closed in the parking lot, but he wished trees swayed outside his window or lawnmowers rumbled over grass. Woods, he'd heard, spread beyond the back courtyard.

On most mornings, grainy sunlight signaled Sheila making rounds. She was tall with solid shoulders and hips, and aside from a few soldiers stationed in Baghdad, Marcus hadn't seen a sister in months.

She reminded him of a girl he'd been thinking of from back home, Kia Winslow, who'd been a long-distance runner, a freshman when Marcus was a senior and the football team's starting tailback. By the time he got home from the medical center, she would be graduating. Would she want to see him? If so, should he smear on makeup?

Nurse Sheila swept into the room Marcus shared with Leroy, stirring the light up with her shadows. (*We ain't have too many sisters in Baghdad,* he often reminded her, saying what Leroy would've said if Leroy could talk.) Sheila was poised to give out meds.

When Sheila neared, Marcus leaned over the side of the bed and fumbled for his cane. He wanted Sheila to laugh, so he raised his eyebrows, and his voice cracked, "You know what they say, don't you?"

She pursed her lips, was all play. "About a man with a long cane?" She looked sideways at him and placed the plastic cup on the stand beside his bed. Pills rattled inside the cup. "Yeah," she said, "he walk with a limp."

Marcus dropped the cane to the floor when Sheila came even closer. She wedged herself between the head of his bed and the nightstand to open the window blinds, and the chestnut skin of her hips and thighs showed through the white fabric of her pants. Her body warmth radiated over his face, and he remembered he'd soon be home.

He wanted to say something to Sheila to explain his appreciation (of her blackness, of her womanhood: it was all very confused), but she yanked open the blinds and moved away. Sunlight slanting into the room illuminated a wall of dust between them.

Marcus's father eased the bronze '94 Ford pickup to a stop beside the gasoline cistern at the end of the gravel drive.

"Let's get you back into commission," his father said, trying to sound upbeat as always, but his grim voice betrayed him. Since he'd first glimpsed Marcus at the Cleveland airport, his father had been brooding.

Marcus's father had inherited the Orwell farmhouse and surrounding one-hundred acres six months earlier from his own father who'd died of a sudden heart attack, though lung cancer had been strangling him for a year. Marcus had the letters telling about the decline. Maybe, he thought, his damaged body looked like his grandfather's had.

The driver's side door creaked when his father slid out. His father shut it, lifted Marcus's duffle bag from the truck bed, and lugged the bag up the cement steps to the front door. His knees trembled, and his face reddened. Even with the wrecked hip, Marcus had shouldered that bag at the airport alone. He smiled at his father's civilian weakness. Then Marcus coughed, and the acridness of the burning city surfaced from his lungs. He'd been hacking it out for months. Is my father, Marcus thought, ashamed of me? He caught his breath and inhaled deeply. White paint on the garage door peeled in fine strips.

The farmhouse still had the original yellow-white siding. Barns with rusted steel roofing stood off to his left, and beyond them, a field that had once flowed with barley lay in clumps of barren, untilled soil. Further back, a honey locust wood and barbed wire fence marked the border where the Norman farm began. Pasture behind the farmhouse stretched half a mile to the edge of the wetlands. The family property had acres of them (a fact his grandfather had withheld from the state), and another hay and barley field spread yellow-green on the other side of the trees, all the way to the dirt and gravel road that separated the farmland and the local gray-stone cemetery. Black oaks at the end of the pasture nodded in wind from over the lake. The lawn around the farmhouse needed cutting. A wood and wire fence marked the northern border, and the fields on the other side of the fence belonged to neighbors he'd never met.

Across from the farmhouse lived a widow, Myrtle Williams. Was she still alive? As a young adult, Marcus had mowed her lawn and raked up leaves in her yard for five dollars an afternoon. Around her century home stretched acres of woods, mainly oaks and elms. A state route passed between their houses. Semis had killed several dogs Marcus's grandfather had owned during Marcus's childhood.

His father shouted from the steps, so Marcus rolled down the window.

"What're you waiting for?" His father's untidy hair tumbled over his eyes. "Let's get some coffee into you." The eyes looked very blue in his pale face.

"You going to have some with me?" For as long as Marcus could remember, brewing coffee meant his father needed to work in his basement office. His father was editor-in-chief of the county's main newspaper, *The Lighthouse*, and it was a presidential election year.

His father threw up his arms. "Of course," he said.

Marcus rolled the truck's window back up, and his image reflected in the side-mirror. The skin on his cheek, where he'd been burnt, flaked and peeled in strips.

That afternoon, Marcus and his father walked down the trail through the pasture. They were going to fish for bass in the pond behind the hay field, but mold had ruined the lines in the poles, so they sat on the dock with bare feet hanging over the water. Deer flies buzzed around their heads and bit through their t-shirts.

On three sides, bare black oaks surrounded the pond. Their large, sharp-pointed buds swelled from branches. Red-brown leaves softened the earth beneath the trees, and directly ahead, an old shack's warped frame leaned to one side. On the open side of the pond, the ground sloped down to the edge of a hay field. The sun shone from that direction. The pond water was too cold to dip bare feet in, but Marcus didn't mind. In the summer, algae blanketed the pond water. Now, it smelled fresh, like rich soil. Marcus sat beside his father while the water reflected the sky. In the reflection, his shadowed face could almost have been the face of someone looking up from the pond bottom.

"Feels strange," Marcus said, "with Grandpa gone."

"He'd be fixing fences this time of year," Marcus's father said. "He'd be chainsawing fallen tree limbs."

When Marcus was a boy, his grandfather had many times given him the early-spring chore of picking up dead sticks. Elated, Marcus would spend entire days combing the woods' floor to load the wheelbarrow. When Marcus was twelve, his grandfather taught him to aim a rifle in order to give Marcus the more manly task of hunting rabbit. Together they'd blasted cans off a sawhorse in the pasture. His grandfather, although born in America, had had Russian parents. When Marcus knew him, he'd had thin wisps of hair matted over his head, very different from his father's tufts. He'd smoked cigarettes and pipes and had always smelled that way, of spicy tobacco leaves. Marcus had never met his paternal grandmother, who was also Russian. She'd died young, when Marcus's father was serving in the Peace Corps in Mexico.

As they walked back down the trail to the farmhouse, his father proposed how to get Marcus *back into commission*. Marcus would rest and do nothing else for a couple weeks, and then he'd start in on light farm work, nothing that would overtax his hip. After a month, he'd choose what was next. His father meant Marcus should decide whether to go back to the university. Too tired to get into that discussion again, Marcus shut up and nodded.

"So rest," his father said as they neared the farmhouse. The mosquitoes were biting, and the sky overhead had darkened to heavy blue.

Marcus stripped in the bathroom. He would take a shower, but first he eased himself down onto the toilet. His bare feet swished over the linoleum floor tiles, and a long mirror on the bathroom door reflected his image. He smirked at himself. What a difference from the alleyways or makeshift latrines (scrape-nests in sand) he'd used back there. In the living room down the hall, his father was still sitting with his feet up in the recliner, watching the nightly news. Marcus massaged his wounded thigh muscles (vastus lateralis, the surgeon had said) while crickets chirped outside the bathroom window. A breeze blew over the pasture and rustled naked tree limbs. He leaned over and swept up a newspaper page, the sports section of *The Lighthouse*, and on the last page, a paragraph announced Marcus's return from overseas. It also featured his statistics from his final two years running tailback for the Ashtabula Panthers: 2,058 yards rushing, 963 yards receiving, 741 yards punt returning, and 10 touchdowns.

What had been his numbers from Kent State? They'd offered him the full-ride to run the ball for their horrid football team but had stood him on the sideline that first year. The team was the worst in the region, pitifully losing almost every game, but still they wouldn't give him the ball. He'd run for over seven-hundred yards that second year, but it hadn't mattered. None of it, finally, made any sense, the games that humiliated him, the classes he'd floundered in because of the hits he'd taken at practice, and the social life. A *liberal* university? Not when he dated that white girl. Anyway he didn't care, so finally he decided to abandon that route for something legitimate. He'd enlisted. And his father had thrown a fit, and now here he was, a maimed cripple. He'd chosen the Marine Corps because that's what he'd wanted, and nobody could've stopped him. Still, shouldn't he have stayed? No, he wouldn't go back. Not in this shape, not in any shape. He'd made his choice and intended to live with it.

After showering, he said goodnight to his father. His father replied, tilting his head forward so that shadows filled the hollows under his eyes. He'd been subdued this entire time, probably steeling himself to put Marcus to work. Marcus walked down the hall to his grandfather's old pipe room, peeled back the over-starched bedding, and slid in. *Can't he just leave me alone for a couple days?*

Marcus reclined in the bed, and his breathing grew shallow. Outside the window, lightning bugs flashed in the backyard and across the acre of pasture. He drove his head into the pillow. He sat up and pressed his hands to either side of his head. He groped to remember what made him feel this way. It was this silence, the open ground between the window and the edge of the field. He scooted himself back, sat against the headboard, and leaned his head against the wall. The stars glowed while lightning bugs flickered. For a moment, he was falling through space. He stopped it by steadying his head with his hands. His father slunk past, the television off, and closed the door to the bedroom across the hall.

Outside, the black-gowned woman crouched against a tree.

Marcus had a nightmare. He was buried under loose earth. His parents and some other people, whose voices seemed familiar, laughed above him. He tried to move, to call out to them, but dirt filled his mouth and he coughed, choking.

He awoke sweating. The odor from the pipe resin made it hard to breathe, so he staggered out of bed and down the hallway to the living room, dragging a bedsheet behind him.

He recognized the nightmare setting. As a child, he'd found a chamber hidden below the church, an underground room that, as part of the Underground Railroad, had once sheltered escaping slaves. He'd opened a wooden door in the wall and had snooped around the chamber alone, the rich smell of soil in the air, but had accidentally locked himself in. He'd stayed imprisoned there for an hour.

What was it I'd found?

In his boxer shorts, he limped down the hallway to the living room, where he fell onto his back on the couch. Floodlights in the driveway cast violet blotches on the ceiling. The woman had gone, but he sensed someone else in the house, someone not his father.

He breathed through his mouth. Deep, measured breathing. He crushed up the bedsheet and hugged it to his chest. His mother would visit tomorrow.

Marcus woke with morning air warming his skin and sunlight slanting through the window. His father had woken early, showered, and opened the windows on his way out the door. Outside, the Ford's engine started, and tires crunched over limestone, and after the truck rumbled back down the drive an hour later, his father hauled bags of groceries through the front door and dropped them by the fridge. He peeked into the living room at Marcus, making Marcus smile. His father had brushed his unruly hair back neatly. Is Dad, Marcus thought, trying to look good for Mama?

Marcus showered, then brushed his hair back the same way his father had done, which gave him a chuckle. Thanks to his mother, his hair had a tougher texture than his father's fine Caucasian hair and stuck up in places like a rooster. The kitchen was astir with sizzling ham and peppered scrambled eggs, and his father wore an apron that, at first, Marcus thought was an undersized dress. His father dashed about, cooking and wiping down counters.

"Where'd you find that apron?" Marcus said. He ran his fingers through his wet hair.

"I'm dicing green pepper and onion for the eggs. Want tomato?" The apron had yellowed over the years and had bluish-red smudges all over it.

His father washed the dirty dishes as Marcus ate. Afterwards, he banged the vacuum cleaner around the furniture in the living room. "Your mother," his father said, "is a very detail-oriented woman." It was true. His mother taught senior-year civics and political science at Ashtabula High, and as far as Marcus knew, nobody had ever passed her classes without knowing (at least on recital day) the Declaration of Independence and the first five paragraphs ("Most importantly the *fifth*," she would say) of Martin Luther King Junior's 1964 Nobel Prize acceptance speech. In the early afternoon, a cobalt blue Cavalier rolled down the drive. His mother had finally come.

She wore her hair pulled away from her face, silver loop earrings, and a purple-blue church dress. Her short-heeled shoes clicked up the steps to the front door, which Marcus opened. He hadn't seen her for almost a year.

Her bronze face had fattened, and her arms were flabby. When she glimpsed his face, she pressed her fingers to her cheeks, leaving momentary fingernail dents under her eyes. Sobbing, she hugged him around the neck. She smelled the same as always, of sharp-scented perfume and blunt powder. Holding hands, they walked together into the living room.

Suddenly wearing a different shirt, Marcus's father perched alert on the piano bench on the far side of the room. He was rubbing his hands over the shirt's wrinkled sleeves. Marcus smirked.

"Hello, Jasheeka," his father said.

"I brought banana bread," his mother said as though it were a greeting. She pressed the warm tin-foiled loaf to Marcus's chest and sniffled, her face all at once serious.

She and Marcus sat next to one another on the couch. She turned her back to the armrest so that she faced him and held his right hand (the unburned one) in both of hers. In spite of his athletic past and military service, his hands were veined and sized the same as his mother's. Then came the questions, her breath smelling of mint gum, about his health. Was he eating? Was he sleeping? Was he eating and sleeping *well*? Yes, he lied.

After the first wave of questions, she scanned the living room and arched her eyebrows. "This place looks the same," she said.

His father sniffed and nodded. He looked out a window. "It'll take some time," he said.

"Perhaps a maid?" she said.

His father huffed out a laugh, and his face reddened. He seemed to hold his breath until he walked out onto the back porch. Marcus laughed through his nose. The reason his parents acted that way, so many years divorced, mystified him.

Marcus's mother, all at once pleased, turned wholly towards him, and they talked well into the afternoon.

"A lot of people been asking about you," she said at one point.

Marcus asked who the people were.

"You remember Kia Winslow?" she said.

"Who wouldn't?"

"She's in the newspaper for getting a scholarship, asked about you just today."

Marcus wasn't sure he could see anybody yet, especially her.

"You look tired," she said after some minutes.

Marcus woke an hour later on the couch because his mother and father were arguing in the kitchen. His father mumbled, and his mother hissed. When they were done, his mother tiptoed into the living room and, after leaning over him, pressed her lips to his mouth. Her lips were chapped. She sat beside him on the couch, with her hip touching his ribs.

"Your old room," she said, "is ready whenever you want it." She meant his childhood room in the basement of the lakefront cottage.

"I'm a couch-man nowadays," he said, patting a cushion, and hated himself for his desire, at least for now, to lounge on the farm. His mother nodded, lips shut tight, and stroked his head.

The next afternoon, nobody answered when Marcus phoned Kia Winslow's house, so he left a message through voicemail. Kia never called back, and after he left one more message, he vowed to let her be. She had probably forgotten about him, but he thought of her every day during his two weeks of sloth, which he spent on the couch or in a lawn chair on the back deck. On the deck, he faced the pasture and stripped naked against the cold spring air.

Once, descending the stairs to the basement to start a load of laundry, he paused at the smell of damp cement. His tongue numbed while, eyelids closed, he returned bodily to the room with earthen walls. As he stumbled back upstairs, he recalled the theatre class he had taken his high school senior year because the theatre had smelled the same way. The class had admitted students as young as fourteen, and in that class, Kia Winslow's shy gaze and trim athletic body had aroused him. By mid-year, he'd managed to hold her hand, once, in the dark theatre. She'd gripped so tightly he thought she'd fracture his knuckles.

On the Saturday morning of Marcus's second week home, the light farm work began. Marcus had to paint the barns and fences. Starting every spring and continuing through summer, the family farm leased out its pastures to fatten cows for slaughter. This year's herd would arrive the following month, so the work, his father said, had to start that afternoon.

His father left him cash and keys to the Ford before descending to the carpeted basement room, where he had a computer and two tables covered with the paper he eclipsed with ink, editing (he said when overwhelmed) the columns of half-literate hacks.

Marcus had to buy baler twine from the mill, and then he'd buy paint in bulk from the hardware store in Ashtabula City, so once in the truck, he eased into first gear and rocked to a stop at the end of the drive. A maddened raccoon emerged arching its back from the weeds while Marcus idled. It stumbled from the long grass, the hide of its shoulders on end, and Marcus left it behind by letting out the clutch and heading down the state route.

Another raccoon crossed the road at the first intersection. It skittered across his path and tumbled into the ditch, and he strangled the steering wheel when, at the same time, a semi barreled towards him in the opposite lane. A bird with blackish feathers had flown in front of the semi and cooked on the rig's grill.

The bird reminded him of a story he'd read in *The Lighthouse*. A week earlier in Harpersfield, a semi on 90 had struck a black bear. The carcass had stopped traffic for an hour before a cleaning crew arrived. Luckily, it had not happened in Orwell Township, where his father served as the cleaning crew (something he'd inherited with the farmhouse), so if anyone hit a coyote, deer, or anything larger, his father would be the one to make a report and take care of the carcass. He buried smaller animals on the spot or chucked the carcasses into the trees with a shovel. If someone collided with a deer, the driver claimed the meat, or his father brought it back to the farm to put on ice. A dozen jars of oily, garlic-saturated venison jerky clinked in the door of the farmhouse refrigerator, and mounted deer and coyote heads overlooked tractors and grease-encrusted tools in the machine shed. As the semi passed, it hurled a pebble that embedded itself halfway into the windshield.

"What do you think, Leroy?" Marcus said. "Sheila like me?"

Leroy's head lolled forward. They'd taken the leg from him and reconstructed the skull. Bandages masked his face.

She survives, Leroy would've said. He was full of morphine.

"Yeah," Marcus said. "She's that way with everybody."

Clouds softened the sunlight while he headed into town. He passed the police station and soon bounced over the muddy parking lot of the mill. After he killed the engine, he inspected the crack in the windshield. It would pitchfork into the dash by winter.

He opened the door and stepped out, and behind him on a telephone wire perched a red-winged blackbird whose feathers gleamed in the cloudy sunlight.

In the medical center in Houston, two other soldiers with leg wounds had healed across from him. One of them, Jim, had always glared at Marcus's writhing. "Jesus," Marcus would groan, pain throbbing in his hip. After a minute of enduring the pain, he would at last feel the mild ache he'd grown used to and give the Puke across from him the middle finger.

Inside the mill, a man whose overalls braced up his stomach squatted on a barrel, and a teenager with a lip swollen with chew leaned against the counter and could've been Jim's twin. Dale, the mill owner, usually stacked the twine by the door, but farmers had already bought what he must've had on the display pallet. Marcus walked over sawdust to the counter and asked if any was left.

Dale beamed at Marcus. "Sam Green's boy, right?"

"I am," Marcus said.

Dale lumbered to his feet and thrust out a hand. "Welcome home, son." He asked the teenager to fetch the twine.

"We read all about you," Dale said.

Marcus knew how to flatter country folk, staying simple and respectful, but what he said he meant. "Good being back."

The teenager stumbled to the counter with a bundle of twine hanging from each hand. He thumped the twine on the counter. "You came to our school," the teenager said, "as a recruiter."

Dale cleared his throat. "This is my nephew. Been thinking about the service."

"You still recruiting?" Dale's nephew said.

"I'm painting fences now," Marcus said, "and trying to get married." He winked at Dale, and the old man grinned.

Back outside, Marcus heaved the twine into the truck bed and started the engine. "*Sam Green's boy*," he murmured. It had been a long time since he'd thought of himself as that. He reversed from the parking spot, put the truck in gear, and headed towards Ashtabula City for paint.

The second time they sawed inches off Leroy's leg, Nurse Sheila carted Leroy back into the room with his face uncovered and the black wire removed from his scalp. Hair sprouted around the groove in the skin where stitches had weaved.

Marcus closed the book of Poe stories he'd selected from the hospital library. "What kind of room they give you?" Marcus said.

Leroy frowned and pointed towards the hallway. "Past the cafeteria, west side."

"Any windows?"

"Could see woods," Leroy said.

"Trees?"

"Trains." Leroy squinted. "A coyote licked the tracks." He turned his head and stared at Marcus for a long time. "What's that mean?" he asked.

Marcus didn't know.

A coyote in a field snarled and flung a snake into the air. The coyote's front legs lifted off the ground. The snake wriggled, suspended.

Marcus and his father drove down the dirt road, deeper into the woods. The Ford rode low from the twenty bales of hay in the truck bed. They were going to deliver them to Fred Dunne, whom Marcus's father hated ("Hyper-liberal, condescending prick," his father'd said). As for Marcus, he hated working with his father. Both of them, when tired from handling seventy-pound bales, waged small wars. His father would bark out orders, and Marcus would take his time stacking the bales and sometimes chuck them on their corners so they burst with pollen and chaff at his father's feet.

The wind had whipped across his face, cold against his sweaty t-shirt, after they'd loaded up the truck. Marcus had stacked slowly, testing out the hip. He'd handled the bales by grounding the bum leg, balancing himself on the good one, and thrusting them with his shoulders. Rain was coming, but the sun had pierced through the clouds enough to make him squint, so they'd left the tarp in the truck cab instead of fastening it over the hay. Halfway to the town of Rome, they drove with open fields on either side of them, and wind gusted and shoved the truck onto the loose soil of the berm. "Damn it," his father said. If it even sprinkled on the load, they'd have to dump it. Moldy hay could sicken a horse, at the worst kill one, and a person like Dunne might sue.

They idled down the dirt driveway and parked beside a red newly painted barn. By the time Dunne, wearing stiff jeans and spotless boots, creaked open the stable's loft door, two rain droplets had fallen on Marcus's arm. Dunne was no farmer, Marcus thought. His painted barn, scarlet mulch around the stable's foundation, and token tractor tire against a tree created a lie: form without function. If anyone had asked Marcus when he was a teenager if he really had a white grandfather who worked a farm in backwoods Orwell, he would've denied it, but even back then, knowing people like Dunne kindled self-realization. He knew, at least, who he wasn't.

Rain slammed down in a torrent on Marcus's last day in the medical center, so hard the hospital sluices overflowed. Brimming ditches flooded the parking lot with water and frogs. Marcus slouched in a chair by Leroy. The frogs below made the parking lot look like the pond behind the Orwell farmhouse.

Jim, the soldier who'd lain across from Marcus and Leroy, had gone home discharged two days earlier and had forgotten a four-ounce bottle of José Cuervo, leftover from a private celebration. Before Marcus caught his taxi to the airport, he would give the tequila to Leroy. He leaned forward in the chair, mulling over what he'd say while rain beat against the window.

Leroy sank into his pillows. Nurse Sheila had raised his bed so that he sat up, and they'd reduced the painkiller dosage enough for Leroy to be able to speak again.

"Hear about Squirrel?" Marcus said. A smell of peroxide and cotton lifted off Leroy's bandaged wound. He meant Sergeant "Squirrel" Reed. "Got his knee capped and was sent home. Bragged he got Sheila's number. Can you believe that? He ain't even half-black." He searched for signs of understanding in Leroy, who should've bantered back over his last words. (Marcus, Leroy had often reminded him, was only half-black.) Had the weeks of mainlined morphine changed Leroy for good?

"Going to your granddaddy's farm?" Leroy said.

"I'll visit you in Texas," Marcus said and, lifting the bottle of tequila, ceremoniously twisted off the cap.

Leroy turned towards him. " '...another draught of the Medoc'?"

"That's right," Marcus said. "Another draught of the goddamned Medoc."

Dunne's stable had two stories. The ground level housed three horses in stalls, and the loft above stunk of horse manure and cat urine. Marcus climbed the ladder to the hayloft, and his father stood in the bed of the truck to heave bales through the loft door.

Marcus waited, the urine stink making his eyes and nose water. He rubbed away tears with the elastic wristband of a work glove.

"Let's go," his father shouted. He'd already dropped a bale at Dunne's feet. Dunne cut the twine with a pocketknife before sniffing and nibbling the hay.

"Do I taste mold?" Dunne said.

"No," Marcus's father said and began slinging bales through the loft door. Marcus took them up and monitored his hip. He slowly slid them behind him and, dragging his bad leg, lugged the lighter ones across the loft floor with one hand. His father would help him stack later, but while he wanted to loaf, it started to drizzle and his father worked feverishly.

"Come on, Marcus, hustle!"

"How wet are those bales?" Dunne said.

Marcus's lungs stung from the ammonia stench. His bad hip stiffened, but his father hurled the bales until they blocked up the door. The loft darkened, and thunder boomed overhead.

"Three more bales, Marcus. Let's move!"

His shoulders burned, and he dug his fingers around the twine to rake back the bales, enough for feeble gray light to reveal to Marcus the rain slanting harder and his father blindly launching the final bale into his chest. Marcus caught it and stumbled back. His father shut the door, and everything blackened. His father would now be taking Dunne's money.

Buried under sweet, prickling hay, Marcus barely breathed, trying to recall what he'd found, when he was a child, in that underground room. It was a shadow, a boy. Someone Marcus knew. *Sam Green's boy*, he thought. *I'm Sam Green's boy.*

CHAPTER 4

Kia Winslow made the front page of Sunday's *The Lighthouse.* "Local Teen Track Star Named Valedictorian." In the color photo, Kia loomed tall because the photographer had taken the shot lying in the grass at her feet. Kia wore her track uniform and a graduate's cap with tassel, and her sleek, long-fingered hands opened over the stunning musculature of her chestnut-colored thighs.

Marcus imagined himself as the photographer, his elbows planted in the soil before her. What will she think of me now? he thought. In his mind, she beamed at him, merciful. But she had never called back. *What does that mean?* It means nothing, he thought. He'd only held her hand once, and that was four years earlier. The thing to worry about was his face. Half his mouth was lipless, a gash in ruined skin.

At the edge of the field by the driveway, honeybees hovered over orchises, and the red and black oaks at the end of the pasture, and all around the farmhouse, had sprouted gleaming green-yellow leaves. He walked towards the Ford with the truck keys jangling in his hand. In the truck, he started towards the lake and his mother. He would go to church with her. He'd try to see Kia, congratulate her, and gauge through her reaction how much he'd changed.

Wearing his old gray-white suit (the coat, now, fitting more loosely around the shoulders than when he'd worn it as a teenager), he drove the Ford northward, and the road, and the trees and fields that flanked him, blurred by. When he'd squeezed Kia's hand in the theatre, her fingers had pulverized his knuckles. The class had been watching a movie version of *The Tragic History of Doctor Faustus,* and earnest weightlifting, the violent collision of bodies on the football field, and his high school popularity had emboldened him. He leaned over in his seat towards the trembling girl. Their lips meshed together, and she jerked away.

Yes, she'd slapped him, but she'd never let go of his bruised runningback fingers.

He approached Lake Road. Behind the lakefront houses, the earth fell away, and the woods thinned out near the water. After he turned onto the road and drove past another line of houses, Lake Erie advanced on his left. As always, when he returned to the lake after an absence, it was as if he'd stumbled upon a reptilian void, a leviathan more space than matter. He gripped the wheel with both hands. " 'Now tell me Faustus, are we not fitted well?'" he recited aloud. He'd played Mephistopheles while Kia had played the Good and (with a costume change involving a furry fedora) the Bad Angel. Marcus laughed out loud. He'd made Kia shriek on stage by tugging her away from the anemic Gill Bithers, who'd played Doctor Faustus. When you're young, he thought, and healthy, almost nothing matters.

Waves broke on shore, approaching at an angle from the northwest. The shallow water rippled brownish-gray. Soon he neared the service road to the cottage community where he'd grown up. At the end of the road, in the driveway closest to the slope down to shore, he parked the Ford beside his mother's Cavalier. He bounded up to the deck but had to steady himself with the guardrail. Greenish mold had softened the wood. He brushed his hand on his pants and rang the doorbell.

His mother opened the door and clasped his hand. She ushered him to the kitchen table and encouraged him to eat.

"I didn't ask if you ate already," she said and pushed his breakfast in front of him, a plate laden with scrambled eggs (salted and peppered), four greasy sausage links, and toast she'd buttered and spread over with jam. He shoveled eggs into his mouth while his mother crushed oranges in her fists for fresh juice.

His mother drove the Cavalier to the house of his maternal grandmother, Marilyn Abrams, who was dying of colon cancer. His grandmother, supporting herself with an oak cane, walked with measured steps down the walkway towards them. Her heavy blue dress fell down her body as straight as a curtain, and she poised her head alertly on her neck.

Marcus's grandmother had visited the farmhouse with his mother the week before, and she'd groaned in his embrace even though he'd hardly touched her.

"We prayed," she'd whispered, her breath hot in his ear.

The roof of the church angled sharply, the gutters hanging three feet from the ground, and resembled an open book dropped facedown in the grass. A playground stretched behind the church into a pine grove that sweetened the air. A train chugged along tracks beyond the trees. His mother parked in the gravel lot, and his grandmother hooked her hand onto the crook of his elbow as they headed for the entrance. The sunshine in his eyes whitened everything around him.

"There's Kia," his mother said, pointing a finger.

In the side yard, Kia wore a white blouse and navy blue skirt, and she knelt holding the hand of a sobbing boy. She inspected the boy's palm before pecking his forehead, and as if suddenly healed, he ran to the swings. Even four years earlier, Kia had monitored the children during the half-hour playtime between Sunday school and eleven o'clock service. The children swung on the swing set, climbed up the stairs of the slide, and loaded buckets with sand in the sandbox. Soon Kia would take the children too young to sit through sermons to the basement.

Marcus stopped at the corner of the church. His mother patted him on the back and smoothly took up the arm his grandmother had hooked on his. He lagged behind as his mother and grandmother moved towards the organ music. At the sound, the children scrambled towards Kia and formed a line. She asked an older child to lead the group through a door that led to the basement playroom. As the children filed down, Kia balanced on the balls of her feet and, scanning the playground for laggards, held the door. Marcus threw his arm out and waved, and she leapt back, the door banging shut behind the last child.

"You scared me," she said. She pressed her hands to either side of her chin. Her forearms were toned, and her neck was slim but muscular.

"Do you know me?"

Kia blinked and shook her head. "Of course," she said and came closer with the elegant steps of a runner. "They put a photo of you in the trophy case. Number twenty-one." Closing her eyes and smiling, she slipped her hands around his back and hugged him. Her hair smelled of coconut oil, and the warm skin of the back of her neck touched his chin.

"Long time ago," he said. She pulled away and looked down. His fingers fumbled at the branch of a lilac shrub. Kia held her hands over her thighs as she'd done in the photo. He should congratulate her, but she spoke first.

"So," she said, smiling again, "can you handle children?"

"What?"

"In the basement," she said. "Think you can?"

"I'm sorry," he said. "My mother and grandmother are waiting." He'd been in the basement as a child and didn't want to go back.

She stepped away from him, suddenly shy. "We'll talk afterwards," she said, "if you can."

"I can," he said, and with a wave, she disappeared down the steps.

Marcus sat at the end of a pew, closest to the wall. Stained glass windows glowed red-orange above and beside him. At the front of the hall, Reverend Byron Jones strolled from behind the pulpit. He had tremendous shoulders and gray shortly cropped hair.

" 'He that hideth his sins shall not prosper,' " the reverend said, looking over his audience.

Marcus turned in the pew. He leaned on the armrest, wood creaking. The reddish strip of carpet, trampled smooth all along the flanking aisle, led to the back of the church. There, underneath the mezzanine, the reverend kept his office, and inside the office lay the hidden panel that led underground. Safety for slaves, terror for him. Other buildings in Ashtabula County had such secret rooms, the Hubbard House for one, just down Lake Avenue.

Soon Marcus realized he was being watched. The man behind Marcus shifted, so Marcus turned to smile apologetically. The man wasn't bothered, but his silver-black face held a sheen, and tears balanced on his eyelids. It was Lincoln Brooks, who used to work the coal docks on Lake Erie, the grandfather of a boy Marcus had gone to school with. Then the woman beside the old man, his wife, stretched out an arm and touched Marcus's shoulder. Her lips trembled. "Welcome back," she said, her head nodding in slight spasms. Behind the elderly couple sat Mister and Missus Metcalf, both teachers at Ashtabula High School, who were also looking at Marcus. He turned to face forward in the pew, and over on the side, two boys sat up straight, proper except for their heads, shyly turned to observe him. Finally Marcus realized what was happening. The elderly folk knew his grandmother, and everyone else in Ashtabula knew his mother, from the dock workers to the recent graduates who hadn't moved away as perhaps they'd planned. In the end, the entire congregation had expected his return.

What did it mean? Who did they think he was? *And how many would guess I've done what I've done, have leapt to the ground at incoming fire and, finding myself wallowing in human remains, burrowed more deeply?*

God forgive me, he thought, but that one stays hidden.

Outside the main doors, Nancy and Kia Winslow stood next to one another in the shade of a poplar. Kia argued with her mother through her teeth, and Nancy stood in front of her gazing towards the exit. As if Marcus's mother knew his thoughts, she addressed Nancy.

"You remember Miss Winslow, don't you, Marcus?" his mother said.

Nancy drove a school bus and on Sundays had always worn vibrant outfits. That Sunday she wore a vivid pink skirt and blazer with shoulder pads. She radiated like a fire beside Kia. Marcus shook hands with Nancy.

"What's wrong?" Kia said. "You look pale."

"I'm good," Marcus said, "just tired." He stood opposite Kia and put his hands in his pockets, then took them out and hooked his thumbs on his belt.

Before he left with his mother and grandmother, he stammered a goodbye.

"Why can't you call sometime?" Kia said. Marcus didn't understand. He'd called twice.

He said goodbye to Nancy, who pressed severe lips together and stared over his head. He should have told Kia he'd already called. What kind of person *wouldn't* call? On his way to the car, he plucked a cluster from the lilac shrub.

The next morning, Marcus woke when his father's alarm clock buzzed at four-thirty. He was sipping coffee in the kitchen when his father, smelling of soap and shampoo, tracked footprints across the linoleum floor.

"You're up early," his father said. He poured a cup of coffee and shuffled towards the basement door but, as if on second thought, dragged out a chair and dropped into it. "Everything in order?"

"I want to finish the barns and fences this week."

His father pushed out his lower lip and nodded. "You'll need breakfast."

"I'll cook it."

An hour and a half later, his father climbed back up the basement stairs, probably after reading email messages and online news. Marcus had showered and dressed before cooking.

"Sorry if they're runny," Marcus said and scraped eggs onto a plate before his father's seat. "Tabasco?"

An hour later, his father pulled from the driveway to go to work, and Marcus stepped from the house with work boots laced up. Across the street, Myrtle Williams' curtains jerked open. The sun inched over the crown of the elm in her yard.

The barn formed an enormous L, and since he'd scraped off the peeling paint on the western side on Saturday, on Monday morning he hit the southern side.

Bill Norman's unfarmed property stood vacant behind him. A high school principal and ex-marine, Bill worked from early morning until mid-evening.

His hip throbbing, Marcus scraped his way to the barn's fenced-in area by noon. Sweat soaked through his t-shirt. He first worked along the feed trough. Afterwards he shuffled along the interior walls, scraping the paint away by hand and climbing a wooden ladder that bowed in the middle when he perched on the top rungs. When thirsty, he guzzled water from a hose in the old milkhouse. He climbed over the wooden fence and sprawled on his back in the pasture to rest. He chewed a blade of bitter alfalfa while the breeze rustled the grass around him.

By three, he had scraped the paint away, so he slunk into the barn's shade and plopped down on a bale. After cooling down, he tugged off the work gloves and rolled off the bale and into a bed of hay. Spiders had wound web-scarves around the overhead support beams.

Tomorrow he would scrape the fences, and he would paint on Wednesday. At that rate, he'd have the second coat on by Saturday evening and could depart for his mother's. He'd sleep on the couch at the lakefront cottage, never again in the basement, in his old room. Kia lived a few miles away.

Marcus told his father about his progress the next morning at breakfast. "Finished the barns, so I'm going after the fences today." He thought of Kia and tapped his finger against his pursed lips. Missing her the day before, when he'd tried to phone while she was out, had made him doubtful. Maybe Kia was only being pleasant, or maybe her mother hated him. He picked at the splinter in the meat of his thumb.

"Good," his father said. "How's the hay?"

"This field's green," Marcus said, "but the one on Foothill might be dry."

"Check, and make sure the barn back there's closed up and still in commission after the rain."

At noon, after Marcus scraped the fence around the barn and swept up paint chips (stupid cows would lap up anything), he limped through the pasture towards the black oaks. The wetlands exhaled cool air. The damned deerflies buzzed him. He should've waited for his father to get back with the Ford.

At the gate at the edge of the pasture, he unhooked a chain and crossed into the wetlands. He fastened the chain behind him and passed along the trail. The air felt moist in his lungs. Brittle leaves crackled beneath his feet on the path wide enough for tractors to pass through with wagons attached. Tractor treads had cut gashes into the soil.

A clearing opened up beside him, where the pond buzzed with mosquitoes and frogs. There, also, the old Russian man's long-abandoned shack and sawmill made a black smudge among shadowed tree trunks. Beside the shack, birds nested in the rafters of the sawmill. Marcus's grandfather had dismantled the saw decades earlier.

Though blackened by weather, the shack soaked up full sunlight all day, and the wood stayed dry. The roof reflected sunlight ruddily. He stepped onto the boards of the deck and pressed his thumb onto the doorknob latch. As the door opened, a stench of rotting wood and animal feces wafted out. The meager room opened ten by ten feet, and on the far wall, spider webs covered a wood-burning stove. Dust floated off a bed frame.

"I checked the hay on Foothill," Marcus said. "Still green."

His father leaned over his plate and slurped up buttered egg noodles. "And the barn?" his father asked and chomped down on a slice of bread.

A barn owl had perched at the apex of the high roof. Marcus had watched it for a long time before locking up. He'd then crossed Foothill and strolled through the graveyard. Behind the graveyard's chain link fence, he'd wandered through fields sprouting purple orchises. A red fox had trotted by.

"The hay looks dry," Marcus said.

After dinner, his father reclined in his chair in the living room and laughed at a televised sit-com. Marcus cleared the table and, it being his turn, washed the dishes. He dried his hands with a rag and lifted the receiver of the kitchen phone. He called Kia, and at last she answered. Hearing her voice made him stutter, but he finally asked whether she'd be at church again that Sunday.

"Maybe we can go for a walk," he said, "around the church."

"Deal," she said, "if you can help me watch the kids."

He said he could and, after hanging up the phone, walked dazed into the living room.

His father was watching the Mexican sit-com *El Chavo* and shook the floor with his laughter.

Marcus reclined on the couch and watched the actor playing Chavo, a youngster on the street who lived in a garbage can. He squinted and stared at a shadow on the ceiling.

"Dad," Marcus said, "do you remember Oscar?"

"Who?" his father said and smiled, ready for slapstick.

"When you took me to the Spanish school, wasn't there a boy?" Marcus said. He almost wished he'd shut up when his father paled.

His father flung his hand in the air and turned towards the television. "Son of a woman we stayed with," he said.

The show continued, but nobody laughed. His father stiffened in the chair. "What else do you remember?" he said and glanced at Marcus.

"I remember getting banged in the head with a shovel," Marcus said. "I remember chasing a ball."

His father's eyes shifted towards the television. "The boy who hit you—" Marcus's father stared at the wall beyond the screen. "It was an accident."

When Marcus left in the Ford on Sunday morning, the farm (according to his father) had never in living memory looked better. The paint had fortified the rickety barn and fences, and the whiteness glared with sudden, clean order.

After he arrived at the church with his mother and grandmother, he found Kia behind the church amid playful shouts. Children in shiny dress shoes raced from the swings to the seesaws, and a boy who'd freed himself of his shoes and pants dug into the sandbox with a shovel. Kia slapped the boy's slacks to knock off sand.

Marcus reached and almost held Kia's hand, but the organ player inside the church depressed a major chord and the children lined up. As she'd done the week before, Kia asked an older child to lead them into the basement. When the line of children had drained down, Kia offered her hand, and he grasped it without thinking. She towed him after the children, towards the basement. He stiff-armed the doorframe.

She turned around and blinked. "You said you'd come down," she said. She stood on the other side of the doorway.

"Stay with me outside?" He tugged her arm.

All the children turned the corner at the bottom of the stairwell. They shouted in play.

"Please," he said. He grasped her elbow with his other hand and pulled.

"What the hell, Marcus," she said. She cringed as though in pain.

He let go. "I'm sorry," he said. "I didn't—"

The organ hit the highest key. His ears rang, and Kia fell back into the church and closed the door. Their gazes met for a moment through the glass before she hurried down.

What have I done? Backing away he collided with the picnic table. The organ music surged through the church walls. He was rubbing the splintered edge of the table when, in the sandbox, the child seemed to squirm.

Get yourself in order, Marcus but the shovel jutted from the sand between two shoes turned upside down. A train behind the pines blared its siren, and his knees buckled at the sound.

The boy in the sand had to be suffocating. Marcus stumbled forward. The train blared over the sandbox and the organ music splintered the church walls. He grabbed the boy's feet. He leaned back, his face towards the drowning sky, and came away with the shoes.

CHAPTER 5

Marcus got an email message from Leroy the next morning. He read the message on his father's basement computer.

Marcus, I got home yesterday. This is my sister Persias computer. She too young for you so don't think nothing. Tomorrow I'm gone to take classes at the community college. I know what you said about that but you got to help. Here is & essay I'm working on for placement can you help me thank you. When you coming to visit? Double-D L

I. Introduction

Remembering starts from childhood till your & adult. You are going to have, these kinds of events your whole life recalling captures your moment & time. Like when some thing suddenly focuses you on a painting rain damaged. No one can steal your photography of what you tasted and think so you can always keep memory scribbled down & if some one loves they will want to buy you a drink or a honey will want to go home with you, etc.

II. Body

I know for my self I can't always keep memory in my thoughts. To try & feel what happened to me three months ago is hard because my recollection has gone blank it's hard to try and recall, so I don't say what I feel I can't think on a clear & straight trail. My mind is always putting sand in a pocket. Writing I always keep a good viewpoint of what really my body tasted and you would be shocked to what comes out my self. Many of today's people do not have the same degree of recollection I tend to believe. There memory's never so real. If you could choose in life you would go for no recollecting. You'd forget you feel from a bridge or sprung & ankle or cut your forehead. When I was growing up most of the time I would hurt my self after I did behave bad & if not caught I blotted it from my mine. When I was a child attend to do wild things & my brain shut down my memory would not except what I do. I blank out the negative and grab with fists the good only for what I have seen & done. but about the MARINE CORPS your memory will come out the pocket like they a hole. I told my buddy. THE ONLY WAY FOR MARINES TO CARE IS KILL YOU START GIVING A DAMN AND WE ALL DAD. We Devil Dogs, man, ASH DOGS. It's what we suppose to DO.

It's really mind boggling because I done a lot a bad and never go back & try to recollect till I don't want to. Many of the thing I done come back & . My mind & recollection GRIEVES. I like this statement because it's a lot you can get from the word GRIEVE because lot's of folk forget that memory with you for life.

The conclusion

basically your memory will out live whatever you do. Writing will help me keep a clear head & straight thoughts.

Marcus leaned forward over the keyboard and held his head in his hands. He'd quit the university two years earlier but knew enough about writing to know his buddy Leroy had little chance of surviving even at a community college. He thumped his fist into a nest of newspaper. Leroy's muddled thinking was his fault. It was his failure to think militarily that caused Leroy to second guess killing the suicidal driver. "By keeping each other alive," Sergeant Squirrel had once said, "we're showing the only sympathy we can afford." But they'd called themselves liberators at first.

He saved Leroy's essay, pressed the reply button, and wrote back.

Leroy, your essay tells truth with feeling. Let me fix comma errors for you. I'll be sending it back proofread tonight. I'll also be visiting you (and the honeys) as soon as I get some change. Heard from any of the others? Phil Michaels wrote, still crazy as a dog. They finally got boxing gloves. Did you hear Squirrel hitched up with Sheila? Not even a bachelor party! Marcus (DDM)

He hit the send button then shut down the computer. He leaned over his father's desk, his chin resting on his fists.

In the middle of the weightroom on base, a duffel bag of sand they'd all beat bare-knuckled had swayed from the ceiling. Marcus had held the bag as Leroy whaled away fifty hooks, and afterwards Marcus had ranted about why he'd quit the football team and university.

"It made more sense in high school," Marcus had said, "when playing made everybody love you." At Kent State, Marcus had rinsed blood from his helmet after every practice. "But what made me leave," he'd said while spotting Leroy's power squats, "was a cracker offensive lineman whose family owned a funeral home. Bitch missed a block at practice on purpose and let the defensive line stampede me. I was knocked out for ten minutes, woke in an ambulance, and for a week couldn't think right in class, and the truth was that was cool with the teachers. They *expected* us to think slow."

He'd quit because those who were supposed to be on his side had betrayed him, and now he wondered if he'd done the same thing to Leroy. If he'd harmed Leroy, he hadn't meant to.

Later that morning, Marcus found his father at the kitchen table.

"Dad," he said and eased himself into the seat across from him, "I want to go back."

"Go back?" his father said. He studied Marcus's face as he'd done the night before, after Marcus had asked about the Mexican boy he remembered.

"I'll take an English class at the Ashtabula campus," Marcus said, "maybe geometry, astronomy."

"I see," his father said and pushed himself away from the table. He turned his back towards Marcus and faced out the window. The sun hid halfway behind the tree line.

Marcus wandered towards his father's room after his father went to work. Until a year earlier, his grandfather had used that room. The rifle they'd shot together used to lie in a white box in the closet. Marcus opened the closet, but the shelf above his father's hanging shirts and slacks held stacks of newspaper. In the far corner was a bottle his father had stashed there. Marcus laughed and reached for it, accidentally stepping on a leather shoe. Dust covered the bottle, and the plastic cap had teeth marks in it. He strode into the kitchen for a glass. His work on the farm, for the most part, had ended, and he was returning to the university he'd shunned two years earlier in favor of militaristic certainty, and he was doing it for at least two reasons. Kia would be there, he knew, but he wasn't sure what he could call his feeling for her. To the town, she was what he'd once been. She was a stagnant city's hope, and everybody loved her.

The other reason to go back was, even from a distance, he had to be with Leroy.

Dust had collected at the bottom of the shot glasses, so he took a coffee cup and twisted off the tequila's cap. He sniffed the liquor, and his gums tingled. He poured a mouthful into a cup featuring Niagara Falls. Then he refastened the cap and slunk back to his father's closet to return the bottle. A stack of newspapers had fallen over into the space the bottle had occupied, so he shoved over the papers to slide the bottle in. While replacing it, he found a cigar box beneath the stack and pulled it out. He hoped it held photographs.

When he opened it, Marcus gasped. He recognized the woman in the first photo. After he closed the box, he passed down the hallway and slid open the door to the back deck. The pasture stretched out before him, and morning sunlight warmed his head and glared over everything. He flipped open the box and stared. She was the mother of Oscar. He tried to remember her name. *Rosa.* She playfully pulled the rim of a straw hat around her face. He lifted the photograph even with the line of trees ahead, and the woman's hair waved around her shoulders and blended into the black oaks.

He knelt and dug into the box. All the photos on the top showed her. His father must've taken them over a span of several years. The deeper he flipped, the younger she grew, and soon photos showed the boy. He'd slammed a shovel blade against Marcus's head when they were kids. Marcus replaced the photos and closed the box, and he slipped his feet into a pair of his father's old work shoes. He stepped from the porch, walking with the weight of the box under his arm towards the pasture, and ducked through the fence to where the grass flowed brown-yellow, the earth tilting towards the Norman farm fifty yards away. Bill Norman was in his backyard on a riding lawnmower. He'd started spring break vacation that week. Marcus had waded halfway out into the pasture when Bill stood from the seat, triggering the engine's emergency shut-off, and waved his arm over his head. Marcus waved back but didn't stop. As he limped across the field towards the trees, his leg pinched where the surgeon had dug.

He ducked and slipped through the barbed wire fence, and finally Bill Norman fired the mower's engine back up. Marcus traipsed through the bed of leaves until reaching the trail, which he took to the shack. He pushed open the shack door and crept in.

The door rocked closed behind him, and he was alone with the recollection of these two people, this woman and boy, and while staring ahead at the stove, he recalled a skillet bubbling with strips of beef in a fatty brown sauce on the burner. It was the kitchen from Rosa and Oscar's house, and behind the stove, out the window, rustled the crowns of palm trees. His father wore an apron and held a big knife. He pushed the big knife away from himself and scraped away sharp needles from ovals of cactus. Seasoned cactus was watery and slipped coolly down the throat.

That afternoon, Marcus crouched on the porch and eyed a low-riding Subaru with tinted windows. The car slowed and pulled into the drive. It scraped bottom, idling towards the house, and Marcus stalked across the yard towards it. Usually unexpected cars meant somebody trying to sell a scam to elderly folk around town, so he flung his arm towards the road and shouted, "Hey!" but the car eased to a stop all the way beside the gasoline cistern and shivered before the engine shut off. Marcus whiffed bitter exhaust. These people never learn, he thought, and he made fists waiting for the driver to step out. The car door opened, and his father popped his head up over the hood.

"Where's the truck?" Marcus said.

His father strode to the rear of the car, nervously fingering a ring of keys in his hand. The rear bumper came up to his knee. He held the keys out to Marcus. "You can't drive the Ford to classes," he said.

"You got me a car?" Marcus said and closed his hand around the dangling keys.

"An investment," his father said. He asked Marcus to give him a ride to the car lot, where he'd left the Ford.

Marcus walked dazed towards the driver's side, opened the door, and lowered himself into the seat. His father's knees came up even with his chest.

"I'll have to get some gravel for the potholes," his father said.

Marcus turned the Subaru around, working the gas and clutch pedal, and stalled at the end of the drive. The front end stuck partway out into the road, but no semis barreled towards them. He started the engine again and accelerated, shifted into second then third gear, and coasted along in fourth. Compared to the cumbersome Ford pickup, the '87 XT Turbo handled like a race car.

"All I said was I wanted to take a class or two," Marcus said. "How'll I pay for this?"

"You as good as have a job," his father said, and he tucked paper money in the elastic band of the sun visor over Marcus's head. The outside bill was a fifty, and there was more than one. "Get yourself clothes."

"What for? Why all of this now?"

"You've got an interview tomorrow."

At a state route, Marcus stopped for the light. The windshield slanted forward at a hard angle, part of a front end that resembled a wooden doorstop.

"You got me an interview?" A semi sped past. The draft shook the car.

"A part-time internship opened up last week," his father said, "and after what you said this morning, and your hard work on the farm—"

"I can get my own interviews."

The light turned green, and Marcus revved up the engine before releasing the clutch. The car lurched forward before spluttering through the intersection. They cruised through half of Rome and all of Morgan Township without talking. In Jefferson Village, Marcus stopped the car opposite the Ford at the used car lot. His father opened the passenger side door, stretched out his legs, and groaned.

"The interview's at ten," he said and shut the door.

Marcus furtively gave his father the middle finger before hitting on the wipers to clean the windshield. He felt as though he lay on his back, wide-eyed, at the bottom of a river.

CHAPTER 6

Gusts blew rain against the lakefront cottage and whipped through window sills. The narrowed wind that leaked through created a howl that, when Marcus was a child, made him believe the house would collapse. After the storm calmed, it drizzled for hours, making the surface of the lake appear to shiver, a vibrating skin. Waves washed timber and glass pebbles on shore. Throughout the storm, Marcus had been preparing himself to visit Kia. He'd driven the Subaru to his mother's house after buying the interview clothes, and now he leaned over the bathroom sink and smeared makeup over his face. The makeup smoothed out the scarred skin.

He'd called Kia's house twice. The first time, Nancy had answered and said she'd give Kia the message. Suspicious, he'd redialed a minute later, and Kia had answered.

"About yesterday—" he'd said.

"Are you sorry again?" she said. "I for*give* you. Can't you have any fun?"

"Of course."

"Tell me why you called because my mother's hissing something."

"I got a car, and tomorrow—"

"Then come get me."

"What about your mother?"

"Can't you take a hint? She don't like you."

Nancy Winslow picked up. "Kia, I need the phone."

They said hasty goodbyes and hung up.

Marcus told his mother he'd be back later and stepped outside. Cool fish-scented wind swept across the lake. The air after rainfall chilled him.

The Subaru tires swished over the wet asphalt as he drove along Lake Road. He headed south after reaching the Harbor and soon neared Kia's street, where two-story homes crowded together on either side of the road. He parked the car and stepped out into damp, pine-sweetened air. The rain had rinsed resin from the pines that surrounded Kia's house.

As he approached, the porch light flashed on. A slippery elm in the front yard gave off a sweet, medicinal scent. In the spring rains, the tree's flower buds had run and reddened the entire tree. He knocked, and a light in the entryway turned on. Nancy Winslow unlocked the front door and opened it. A security chain pulled taut across her face.

"You?" Nancy said. A crimson handkerchief stretched around her head.

"Kia invited me."

Nancy inspected him. He wore an ironed pair of slacks and a cotton shirt, and his hair was cut short and parted neatly. She pushed out her lips and scowled, then closed the door. The chain rattled, and she yanked the door open again to let him pass. She wore a nightgown and rubbed a dishrag over her hands. She relocked the door behind him and, with her arms dangling at her sides, walked stiffly into the kitchen as though exhausted.

Kia tiptoed down the hall with a blue handkerchief on her head. She held her hands in front of her chest, fingers interlocked. Marcus again smelled coconut oil.

"Ready to go?" she said, looking up at him.

Nancy slammed a cupboard door closed, and Kia's eyes flashed towards the kitchen, then back to Marcus.

"Why don't you two come into the kitchen?" Nancy called. "Marcus, you want coffee?"

"Be back later, Mama," Kia softly said while opening the door.

"What?" Nancy lumbered from the kitchen, staring not at Kia but at Marcus. "Where do you think you're going?"

Kia pulled Marcus outside by the wrist.

"Kia!" Nancy called.

Retreating, almost making him plow through daffodils along the walkway, Kia called back over her shoulder, "It's only Marcus."

Nancy appeared in the doorway. "But the boy wanted coffee!"

Marcus opened the passenger side door, and Kia shouted, playfully simple, "See. He opened the door for me."

A dog barked at the bedlam, and soon two more dogs along the street barked.

Marcus slid in.

"Are you sure this is all right?" he said.

"I'm eighteen and this isn't church," she said as though to someone on the sidewalk. "And you're safe, right?" She looked at him. The handkerchief framed her face and intensified her mouth.

Marcus started the engine. "Repent," he said, sooner than he'd planned, "and your mama shall never raise thy skin."

"That's my line!"

Fifteen minutes later, at the lakeside park, he crept the Subaru down the path with the headlights off and parked in front of a post and wire fence. Kia swung open her door and eased herself onto the car's front end. Marcus pulled himself from the driver's seat and surveyed the park, which was officially closed. Satisfied they'd be alone, he walked to the front of the car and sat beside her. The ground on the other side of the fence sloped to the water, and a breeze cooled his face.

"I read you'll study nursing," he said.

She shrugged. "That's what my mother wants."

Park lights lit up her profile. Her lips pouted. "She's trying to keep you safe," he said.

She crossed her arms, her hands clutching her ribs. "She's trying to keep me bored."

"Then what *do* you want?"

She turned towards him as though she'd scream. He flinched when she snatched up his hand and dragged him towards the footpath down to shore. He'd just bought the slacks, but he skidded down the slope regardless.

Waves broke in front of them, and rushing water churned and fizzed before another wave lapped onto the sand. Kia slipped off her shoes and pulled her legs from her jeans. She left her t-shirt on. Marcus knelt down to pull off the Italian shoes he'd bought and dropped the new slacks on them. He had the interview tomorrow, but with Kia stripping beside him, new slacks meant nothing.

41

He stood in his boxer shorts, goose bumps rising on his arms and chest. The wind over the lake was chilly after rainfall. Kia shuffled towards the water and squeaked when a wave swished around her feet. Her skin gleamed gold-brown in the moonlight. The water foamed around her ankles then sank back into an undertow. Marcus waded out, with slippery stones hardening the first stretch of the shallows. He and Kia used each other for balance, and Kia fell towards him and clutched his arm with both hands. Water rose over his thighs, and soon their feet meshed into soft sand. Water rippled beneath their chins. The water balanced him, and for some time he and Kia smiled at each other, heads bobbing as waves lifted and dropped them back to the sand.

"So you *can*," she said.

"Can what?" His teeth chattered.

"Have fun."

He lifted his knees to his chest and threw them back down to the sand before his body sank. His left hip pinched, so he planted that leg and lifted the good one and kept warm. He wondered what Kia's body was doing underwater.

Returning to shore, they slipped over the stones, and Kia gripped his arm for balance.

"I'm going back to school," he said.

"My mom should hear that."

On the beach, she turned to him and came close.

"What is it?" he said. His hand shot up to his face.

Kia stretched out her arm and rubbed her thumb over his cheek. The water had washed off some of the makeup.

"There," she said. She stepped back to observe her work. "Better."

Marcus swallowed, then lunged forward. He wrapped his arms around her waist, but she wrenched herself free.

He blinked at her raised hand. She shook her head. "That's not how it's going to go," she said.

After his mother went upstairs to bed that night, Marcus received a phone call from Bill Norman.

"Seen you this morning," Bill said, "but couldn't get you to come and talk."

"I didn't understand," Marcus said.

Bill Norman had been Marcus's summer baseball coach in Orwell, and he was the type of man who inspires boys to scorn everything feminine.

"So when you going to come by the school again?" Bill asked.

"When my face stops scaring kids," Marcus replied. Although Kia had held his hand tightly when he'd dropped her off back home, he might've ruined his chances with her.

"You all right, son?" Bill said. "Never heard you—"

"I don't recruit anymore, Mister Norman."

"I know that," Bill said, and he reminded Marcus of the elementary children who'd sent thank-you letters to Marcus's platoon. "They'd appreciate a guest speaker, and everyone at the high school knows you since they put your picture and football jersey up in the trophy case."

The windows facing the lake glared back his reflection. He had dark cavities beneath his eyes. If this was the type of man Bill Norman wanted to speak to children—

"Marcus? You there?"

Marcus had agreed to visit the schools the next day, and after they hung up, he crossed the living room to dig into the duffel bag. He found the Purple Heart. (Marcus had waddled using the cane, but Nurse Sheila had needed to roll Leroy in a wheelchair for the ceremony. They both wore Marine Corps t-shirts, and an American flag blanket hid Leroy's legs. In a conference room, a poster of a model marine holding an M-16 hung behind Marcus. He stood before nurses, wives, friends, and parents. Nobody from his family had come because he'd never told them. A pink-faced major with brown blotches over his forehead had breath that smelled of ham. His milky face was droopy and pitying as he stabbed the medal into the neckband of Marcus's t-shirt. Marcus held the certificate for the photographer. The medal stretched the elastic neckband out. The shirt never fit right again.) Marcus let the medal go and crawled over to the living room couch for sleep. He would speak to the children, yes, but in plain clothes and as a civilian.

The alarm clock woke him at six, and he stood up from the couch and stretched. Seagulls glided over misty water to feast on fish the storm had washed on shore.

He showered then ironed his slacks in the living room, flicking off sand. After he'd dressed for the interview, he dug into breakfast.

The bitter coffee his mother brewed reminded him of mornings from childhood. His parents had sipped coffee and read at opposite ends of the kitchen table while, in between them, he'd slurped oatmeal from a spoon. His mother had always left first and turned the television to the weather channel or local news. Sometimes he'd behave wildly and run from room to room shrieking like a seagull. He must've been six or seven because his first grade teacher had sent him to the principal's office for doing it: at the end of the school day, he'd lagged behind as his peers filed out to the buses, and alone in the classroom that had bustled all day, he shrieked his high-pitched seagull imitation and listened in a thoughtful trance to his echo. His teacher had caught on and waited in the hallway to punish him, but at home, the screams had doubled over his parents as he'd glided from room to room.

"What are you smiling about?" his mother asked.

"What was it Dad used to read in the morning?" The sun hung dull gray through the mist over the lake. "When I was a kid, he read a newspaper in Spanish."

"*La Jornada*," his mother said. "What made you think of that?"

In the cigar box, there'd been photos, dozens of them.

"I don't know," he said.

His mother clinked her cup into the kitchen sink and, after squeezing his shoulder and kissing his forehead, gathered her purse and keys to go to work.

At nine o'clock, Marcus parked across from Kia and Nancy's house. He was just going to pass by but had to stop when a police cruiser was idling in her driveway. The cruiser pulled from the drive before Marcus could ask what had happened, but Kia was standing in the front door as he walked up. "I just tried calling you," she said and locked the door behind him.

"What's wrong? Why aren't you at school?"

"Someone was outside my window last night," she said.

"Who?"

"A stranger. I heard crunching in the grass, and I turned off my desk lamp and saw him."

She told him the story over and over at the kitchen table. She'd been studying, and the prowler had cut the bottom of her window's screen with a knife or razor.

Marcus agreed to inspect the backyard for her before he left, and then promised to return after the interview. He checked the line of pine trees on either side of the house. Back in the front yard, he adjusted his tie, unbuttoned his blazer, and when she waved through the window, he signaled that he'd found no signs by giving a thumbs-up.

Marcus hurried past the juvenile detention center, a tall brick building attached to the courthouse. He imagined youths in bright orange jumpsuits in the windows watching him near the building *The Lighthouse* leased, a three-story box. The sun beat against his head and made him sweat beneath the blazer, but the air-conditioning refreshed him as soon as he entered the lobby.

Mirrors formed the lobby ceiling. He stood waiting for the elevator between two pillars. He read on an information board that his father's office was located on the second floor, Human Resources on the third. A tall man in a white shirt, a gold watch and eyeglass frames, stood beside him. The man wore a tie, no blazer, and waited for the elevator, which slid open without a sound. Gold railings wrapped around the inside to keep people from leaning against the mirrored interior. The tall man looked down at Marcus, and even though they alone occupied the space, neither spoke except when the man asked which floor Marcus needed.

"Third," he said.

The man pushed the button. Paper hung from his hand, and Marcus smelled cologne and felt as though the man was looking him over. The elevator stopped at the second floor, and two women walked in. Their smiles turned to awkward gaping when they noticed his face, and they looked at the ground and twirled around in the elevator to face forward. His grotesque reflection gazed back at him from the mirrors.

The doors opened at the third floor. The two women walked out first, and he limped from the elevator and down the hallway next. The wide-striding man holding paper passed him and burst through the door at the end of the hall, just behind the two women.

Soon Marcus eased open the door and stepped up to the counter. Behind it the tall man massaged the shoulders of the receptionist then, glancing at Marcus, sank back into the cubicles. The receptionist cleared her throat and sat upright in her chair. She had deep wrinkles around her eyes.

"I'll be right with you," she said. Her fingers rattled over the computer keyboard. "Now," she said, "what do you need?" She glimpsed him and looked away, blushing.

"I've got an interview," he said, "with Mister Johnson."

The woman looked at his chest, and her voice came soft and wispy. "Are you here for the janitorial position? Maybe you want *Lionel* Johnson?"

"A copy editing internship," he said. He wasn't going to say who his father was. He also wasn't going to forget the way everyone around him behaved. *Always remember*, his Grandma Abrams had said, *the way they greet you at first and leave you for good.*

"I'm sorry," the woman said, still not looking, "the position's been filled."

He read the name-plaque on the woman's desk. *Georgia Bimm.* That name sounded familiar. Behind the woman, the tall man from the elevator walked past with his hand on the shoulder of a stocky yellow-haired man with a buzz cut. Like Marcus, the stocky man wore a blazer. The men filled their chests up with air as they shook hands, and the buzz cut walked behind a cubicle but soon appeared again holding paper in his hand. He waved fat fingers at the receptionist but turned blank the moment he glimpsed Marcus. Something about his face made Marcus frown.

The young man plowed through the glass door and held his arms out at his sides.

"What did you say about Mister Lionel Johnson?" Marcus said.

"Did you want to see Lionel? He's in the basement," she said. "Did you see the service elevator when you came up?"

At last Marcus remembered what the woman's name reminded him of. She had the same last name as the offensive lineman who'd missed the block at practice two years earlier, letting the left side of the line dog pile him.

"Excuse me," he said, "but is your son's name, by any chance, Vernon?"

The woman looked. "No, my nephew's is. You know him?"

"He must've just graduated, right?" He knew how to talk to white folk. "I played ball with him."

"Actually," the woman said, and she pointed a pink-nailed finger down the hall, "*that* was Vernon."

Marcus followed Vernon, and in the hallway, he poked the button for the service elevator while Vernon smiled to himself. The doors of the main elevator opened.

"Get some good news?" Marcus said.

Vernon stared at the floor, snorting as he strode into the elevator. He leaned against the far wall to give Marcus room to enter and push the button.

Marcus smirked. *He doesn't recognize me.* The main elevator closed, and Vernon was gone.

Behind him, the doors of the service elevator shrieked open. The elevator quivered as he stepped in. When the doors closed, deep scratches in the metal disfigured his image. He pushed the button for the basement, took off the blazer, and flung it over his shoulder. The elevator descended to the bottom, where the door opened to a cool puff of damp basement air. Marcus walked along a chain-link fence of storage area. On the other side someone had heaped manual and electric typewriters. Ahead, a radio played NPR. He smelled coffee. At the end of the hall, a boiler hulked in front of him, and an old man reclined in a desk chair beside it.

"Can I help you, young man?" Although the man's shoulders hunched forward, his forearms swelled inside the loose ash-brown skin.

"I'm looking for the exit, Mister Johnson."

The old man lifted a weary hand.

CHAPTER 7

As Marcus neared the school, the building reminded him of the dormitory they'd camped in after the invasion. In convoys, he'd ridden to and from it, and when reporters rode along, one from Nairobi had begged to return after they'd passed a bridge where boys had tripped into cluster bombs and smeared the asphalt. Marcus was scheduled to talk to schoolchildren from the elementary school that afternoon, and afterwards he would visit the high school. The children had sent his entire unit letters. On the couch at the lakefront cottage the night before, he'd tossed at the ache in his hip after clasping the Purple Heart. In the meantime, he had tried to plan something to say and had managed to scribble a few notes on an index card in the morning.

He walked through the storm doors and rang a bell outside a bulletproof window. He slid his driver's license through and signed in. Then he scribbled his name on a nametag sticker and slapped the sticker onto his chest. The receptionist hit a button, and security doors buzzed.

Out in the hallway, students babbled in line and bumped into one another, filing into the gymnasium. One chubby boy with a torn collar waved. Marcus waved back, which encouraged another boy to flail his arm over his head and shout. Marcus turned into the main office to wait for Bill Norman.

He slipped off his shoe and held it upside down. A lake pebble clicked on the floor, and a boy beside him giggled. The boy had an Indian accent and asked Marcus what had happened to his face.

"A dragon kissed me."

"Ew," the boy said and pinched his nose. "Your foot stinks."

During boot camp, swamp water had soaked through their socks and into their boots. In the waterproof boots, their feet had pickled and, at the barracks, reeked of basement mold.

Bill Norman marched into the main office.

"Morning, Private," Bill Norman said. He wore a gray suit.

They shook hands and walked towards teachers mingling outside the gym. Inside, the children shouted, and their voices echoed.

"Are you ready?" Mrs. Scullion said. Wilma Scullion, Marcus's first grade teacher, had busted him for squawking in the empty classroom sixteen years earlier. She still hunched taller than him, nearly a foot, and her face looked sunburned.

"I hope so," he said. He flapped the index card under his chin as if it were a fan. The teachers around him giggled.

"We're really glad you came," another teacher said. He had a black goatee, and Marcus had never met him before. "It's just great."

Bill Norman, who'd been watching Marcus, pulled his hands from his pockets and tilted his head. "What do you think?" he said and tapped Marcus's nametag with his fingers. "Ready for the show?"

Bill winked, straightened his back and shoulders, and hushed the gymnasium by entering it. While Bill walked away, Marcus wished he'd slapped him on the shoulder. It *was* a show. The university had sickened him, but he'd learned, most clearly at recruit graduation, that even the Marine Corps fed people spectacles. Marcus and all the other recruits had stood during the Emblem Ceremony, their family or friends in the crowd, and while their drill instructors had stepped down the line, the guy next to Marcus had bawled. When at last an instructor stuck the pin onto Marcus, Marcus had sneered to show he knew what this was. It was pre-game prayer or the anthem before football games.

Bill walked in front of a podium on stage and adjusted the mike. An American flag hung on a wooden pole beside him. After clearing his throat, he introduced Marcus, a former student at the elementary school. Raising an arm, he beckoned Marcus forward.

The kids clapped as Marcus mounted the steps to the stage. The children had taped pieces of paper on the walls of the gym, each piece depicting a water scene. Blue, black, and gray swirls of water surrounded him on all sides, and the children in front of him wiggled in rows. They all stared. Bill Norman gave him the mike and stepped offstage, but instead of sitting down, he stood with hands clasped before him at the foot of the steps.

"On April fourteenth last year," Marcus began, "you adopted my unit." Children whispered, and Wilma Scullion fiercely shushed them. "Since I was once a student myself here, it touched me that you'd sent us cards." All the way in the back, behind the students, the teacher with the black goatee aimed a video camera mounted on a tripod. A red light blinked. The surface of the children slanted downward towards the stage, and the children in the front crossed their legs on the floor. Two girls twirled each other's hair while the Indian boy from the office sat up straight, his long hair in a bun. Another boy fingered his shoes to activate red lights in the soles. The boy next to him spun a plastic handgun on his finger.

"Without mail call," Marcus said, "we would've never made it. A lot of guys tuck those letters into their fatigues. I don't know why. You don't want to think about home. Or, not in the wrong way. The wrong way is when it hurts someone." He gripped the podium with both hands. It was hollow. He leaned over and tipped it forward. It banged square on the stage when he let go. "I knew a guy who tucked one letter beneath his flak jacket and said it reminded him he saved kids back home. He had to think that because that was the right way. The wrong way—" Bill Norman swayed beside the stage. Bill's cheeks had reddened, and the tip of his tongue swept over his upper lip. "They're building all over Baghdad. I guarded a site for a children's hospital, the biggest hospital I'd ever seen. With the letters, you might remind a guy you replace any child who dies. Without them, a marine might think that in order to be forgiven he'd have to raise the dead."

The teacher with the goatee jerked his head up from the camera, and Wilma Scullion leapt from her seat.

Bill Norman's face swelled red as he stumbled up the steps.

"Thank you," Marcus said.

That evening, Marcus's father phoned that he'd be home late from work. Marcus crouched forward on the couch while the sun set and dozed off until the floodlights turned on. The lights cast violet stains on the ceiling.

We stumbled hacking to the outside away from the building and air cooled and stung and between Leroy and me she sprawled. I did it with my rounds collapsed the white soft stomach caved in. She's Rosa on the ground in the dust that's Rosa.

Where was his father? Marcus paced across the room and realized he'd dozed for only half an hour.

He tripped down the hallway in the dark, and in the kitchen he switched on the light. The dim bulb shed thin gold. With the kitchen phone he dialed Kia's number but nobody answered. Nobody answered at his mother's either, so he snatched the keys off the table and pushed his feet into the boots. Dozing off had confused him. He leapt past the basement door and paused outside.

On the porch, he slouched against the house. He caught his breath, the evening air sweet with pine needles. The pines reached up into violet shadows.

"What you sulking about?" Leroy had asked. "Will you just press the damn weight?"

Marcus had leaned forward on the bench, and Sergeant Squirrel Reed had swaggered in. Squirrel heaved barbells in each hand and wheezed curling them. He grimaced at himself in a mirror. With every repetition, the weights thumped against his chest. The woman and Rosa, they had the same black hair.

Towards Kia's house, high dusty weeds in the ditches narrowed the roadway. In Ashtabula, he idled past the house. All the lights were off. He depressed the gas pedal and sped along Lake Road, the lake breaking down the earth on his right, and at the service drive, he turned and drove towards the lakefront cottage. His mother had taken the Cavalier somewhere. He parked anyway and knocked on the door. The porch light was on.

He drove back into town. His grandmother would still be awake. She'd invite him in and boil water for tea. She'd chat with him at the kitchen table or in the living room, maybe serve him dessert.

He parked in front of his grandmother's house and walked to the side door. He knocked, but even she had gone somewhere. He waited, scanned his surroundings. Nobody. After he hammered his fist against the door again, he stalked off into the residential alleyways, through backyards, startling dogs on chains or behind fences. When he came to train tracks, he crunched along the tracks and left the streetlights behind. The tracks wound behind the residential blocks, and frogs croaked in flooded ditches and low-lying pools. His feet kicked up an oily earth smell from the cinders. Far ahead, a train blared its horn, so he skidded down the bank and walked along a passageway between a fence and the wall of a fertilizer plant. He'd been there before. The block ahead was where Kia lived.

He cut back between houses and ducked under tree limbs. He crashed through shrubs, the damp grass soaking through his boot toes, and he stopped at the scent of pines. Needles crunched under his boots. In front of him stretched a wide wall. This was Kia's backyard, and the wall was the back of her house.

I shouldn't be here. He searched for a way to escape, but something in front of him shifted in the needles. He dove deeper into the pines and hushed. Through the tree trunks, a smear of bluish-gray shifted. A silhouette of a woman. "Who?" he whispered, but he knew. He'd murdered her in Baghdad. She wanted to know why.

Brilliance burst over the yard when Kia flipped on her light and flung aside the curtain.

Marcus gripped the sticky trunk and held his breath. Kia's hand spread open against the glass as though reaching.

Bill Norman had called and asked Marcus to talk to a few high school boys. After Marcus's speech at the elementary, Bill had followed Marcus to the parking lot. He'd dropped his arm on Marcus's shoulder and sent him home, but he'd phoned the next morning. (To get it over with, Marcus thought.) "Just give them the facts," Bill had said. Mister

Norman wanted Marcus to talk about the financial and physical rewards, and Marcus would, but he wasn't sorry for the elementary school scandal. He'd accidentally said too much, but all of it was true.

The rain pounded on the Subaru roof and sounded like hurled clumps of dirt. At the church, he parked between the reverend's Cadillac and Bill's Dodge pickup, splashed across the gravel to the main doors, and ducked under the awning. A young man (likely one of the high school kids he'd talk to) hunched his shoulders and sucked on a cigarette. He was taller than Marcus, had freckles on his nose and cheeks, and wore a baseball cap. One of the young man's blue eyes peeked from under the bill when he nodded, exhaling blue smoke. Marcus entered the church vestibule. Rain tapped on the roof, and a similar sound came from the corner of the dark room. It was hip-hop jangling from a pair of headphones. Another young man crouched in the dark, his baggy pants looking like a loose sack around his legs. His arms dangled forward between his raised knees, and his shoulders and neck bobbed to the beat. He lifted one hand in front of his face as though rapping, but the darkness of his skin and the room obscured the features of his face.

The young man tugged the headphones from his ears and dropped them around his neck. He stood up. He was stocky and naturally muscular, would be a heavyweight marine even after basic. He clasped his beltline with one hand and reached to shake with Marcus.

"Here to recruit us?" he asked. Young Buck banged from the headphones. "My name's Robert."

Marcus nodded and said his name.

The other teen came in from outside, his boots clomping over the floorboards. He stunk from smoking in the rain, his whole body saturated with tar. This kid was the same height as Robert but skinnier. Both boys had pants so large they hobbled, and each had headphones fettering his neck.

"I'm Todd," the thin teen said.

Reverend Jones called from the congregation hall, waving an arm, so Marcus led the boys down the carpeted aisle between the pews. The reverend held the door open and said Principal Norman was waiting in the first room on the left.

In the narrow, low-ceilinged hallway, oil paintings depicted scenes from Christ's life. As the boys moved down the hall, Christ grew older. Robert snickered beside Christ lugging a splintered cross and murmured, almost spitting the first syllable, "*Prin*cipal Norman." After Christ (now blond and fair-skinned) floated over the heads of awed friends, Marcus arrived at the meeting room where Bill Norman was waiting. Bill leaned with his elbows planted in front of him at the head of a table. He wore a shirt, tie, and blazer. He had two folders in front of him, one thin and one thick with paper, and beside him a stack of Marine Corps pamphlets. At last Marcus realized how these teens had come to be here. They were troublemakers, and Bill had given ultimatums.

Both boys sat at the end of the table, far from Bill. Robert dragged his chair out and slumped into it, legs spread apart and almost reclining, while Todd chewed his lower lip and eased himself into a seat, one elbow on the chair's armrest and his closed fist pressed against his ear. Marcus lingered by the door.

The room was used for Sunday school. Low book shelves held hardcover Bibles, crayons, stuffed animals, and blocks. A square wooden door made an impression in one of the walls. It was the entrance to the underground chamber.

"Aren't we missing a boy?" Bill Norman said and lifted a folder that held a single sheet of paper. "Anyone seen him?"

Todd perked up and said he'd go check. Bill's face reddened, so Marcus said he'd go and hurried away, not waiting for a reply.

He passed through the doorway to the congregation hall and stopped. At the back of the hall, wind howled through the open door of the vestibule. He walked down the aisle between the pews and pushed the door open. Raindrops sprayed against his face, and a breeze permeated his shirt. Another car had arrived outside, so the missing boy had probably just come. Marcus closed the door and crossed the hall towards the reverend's office.

Inside, yellowed parchment ruffled in a pile on a desk. Webs strung between the feather of an antique quill and the room's crimson woodwork, and robes hung in a closet. He turned around in the reverend's doorway and listened. Nobody, so he closed the door and walked over to the closet, where he swept aside hanging robes. He reached back, wooden boards narrow on either side of him, and touched the wall. The panel was loose, and at that realization he trembled. He tried to control his breathing but huffed. This was something he had to explore. He'd found something there the last time.

He burrowed past the robes and pushed on the panel. When the panel sprung open, air that smelled of rich soil puffed out. Marcus gripped either side of the woodwork around the entrance and felt for the wooden steps leading down. They were still there but rotting. He fumbled on his left side and raked his hands along the crumbling earthen wall. He then crept down the steps while holding his breath, staring wide-eyed into the blackness. Breathing through his mouth, with the rich smell of clay damp in his lungs, he found himself alone.

Last time he'd been there, he'd thoughtlessly pulled the door closed behind him and, trapped, had scraped against the exit trying to escape, driven by an understanding he could be abandoned. *Like mothers, sons were sometimes left for good*; it was a lesson his father had taught him in Mexico.

But there was something else he'd learned there.

I'm not the only son, he'd realized, *and Mama's not the only mama.*

Marcus backed the Subaru into the farmhouse turnaround and killed the engine. Beside him, the light at the top of the splintered pole glowed dull yellow. Moths fluttered around it. He sat with the seatbelt snug around his shoulder, his hands loose around the steering wheel.

Down in the basement, his father would be working. They'd almost never talked freely, so going down now would likely lead to both of them storming away flush-faced. He hated the idea, but he needed to know whether the injury, or time, had caused him to forget that Oscar was his brother.

He unbuckled himself and opened the car door. Crickets clicked in the grass, and lightning bugs flashed. He shut the door and crossed the drive. When he'd climbed the porch steps, he unlocked the door and stepped into the foyer. He flipped on lights before entering the kitchen and stopped at the top of the stairs. Below, his father's fingers rattled over the keyboard. Marcus gripped the rail and took a step. The typing stopped as Marcus went down.

All the lights in the basement were off except his father's desk lamp.

"How'd it go?" his father said but squinted at something on the desk. In the middle of a stack of papers stood a coffee cup featuring Niagara Falls. The tequila was still inside, and a cigar box lay closed beside it.

"I'm sorry," Marcus said. "I snooped, I don't know why."

His father nodded, staring at something on the desk. The lamplight made him look elderly.

Marcus cleared his throat and stood up straight. "When we went together, when I was a kid, it was to see Oscar, my brother."

Slumping at the desk, his father tilted his head to one side. He didn't look.

"When did I forget?" Marcus said. "Was it the injury?"

"No," his father said. "You slowly stopped mentioning him, over time."

"But why?" Marcus said, louder than he'd planned. "Why did I forget? If we weren't going to go back, why take me at all?"

"That's no way to talk," his father said, his glassy eyes rolling towards him.

Marcus almost asked if his mother knew, but, now, the reasons why his parents divorced were clear. "I understand," Marcus said. "You weren't going to come back. That's why you took me."

"Marcus, sit down."

"I can't." He limped to the stairs and pulled himself halfway up. "I'm sorry."

"Marcus, stop!" His father staggered from the desk, brushed against a stack of newspapers, and shuffled forward with a letter in his hand. "Talk's no good," he said, "and I'm too settled to change." He stretched out his arm, and Marcus took the envelope.

"What is it?"

"Guilt cripples," his father said and tucked his hands into his pockets. "Guilt keeps jobs from getting done."

Marcus slipped the letter into his back pocket. "I don't know," he said, but his father's gaze had strayed to the floor, so he mumbled a goodbye and climbed the stairs. In the foyer, he stopped, wondering if his father would be typing again, but he heard nothing.

In Ashtabula, he parked the Subaru outside Kia's house and tore open the envelope. His father had folded a sheet of paper around photographs. Marcus unfolded the letter, written in a narrow hand.

Regret hobbles us, and someone, whatever our choice, always struggles. So I had to accept making two families; next I had to decide what to do. I chose logically and ethically to stay with the family in the country where I was born and where I earned enough to provide for everyone. I suspect you will want to see Oscar. If you go, go knowing I sent money every month until he was eighteen. Occasionally, I sent money afterwards, but Oscar's made trouble for himself. He's changed from the boy you briefly knew. He lives in Mexico City, away from his mother, who long ago married. I don't know what the hell Oscar does. Now, my living closer might have made Oscar different, but what about you? Here's Rosita's number, 001-52-777-321-0000, and here's her address:

Rosita Rodríguez Castro
Privada 3, Col. Progreso
Cuernavaca, Morelos, 60000

After he placed the letter and photos in the map compartment, he stepped from the Subaru and walked down Kia's drive. She pulled the curtain aside in the front window as he passed along the walkway. He waited on the porch, cicadas rattling around him. Kia cracked open the door, grasped his arm, and shushed him.

"Try to walk quietly." She locked the door and tugged him down the hall. They tiptoed past Nancy's door.

Once he entered the sweet-smelling space of Kia's room, lit by a lamp, she shut the door and took him to the window. Beside him spread her bed. On her desk, lilac flowers lolled in a vase.

"What is it?" he said.

"Can't you see?" She stepped to the wall and flipped on the ceiling light. After she snuggled next to him, she pointed at the window.

He leaned forward, and his reflection gained definition. Kia pushed up beside him so that both their reflections hovered. She scrutinized his image, like someone studying a mug shot.

"I see us," he said.

She interlocked her fingers with his and reached to close the blinds. Safe from anyone's view, they reached for each other. "Anything else?" she said.

He dared again to lean forward. Watching, she slid her hands around his neck to pull their mouths together.

Cupping her hips, he turned his face. "The light," he said.

She laid a hand on his mouth, her fingers salty. "I want to see."

BOOK 2

MAKERS OF WRECKAGE

One thought. fills immensity.
William Blake, 'Proverbs of Hell'

CHAPTER 1

After changing buses in Columbus, Marcus slouched with his elbows on the cushion of the back aisle seat. His body quivered while the bus barreled westward along the highway. Around him, most passengers had shut the plastic eyelid over each window and become slumping silhouettes.

A woman boarded in Richmond. She swayed down the aisle, disturbing beams of light from streetlamps, and Marcus gasped. Fire seemed to have burned away the woman's lips, but as she neared, he realized she'd only been weeping. She slid into the opposite aisle seat one row in front of him.

When the bus had merged with highway traffic, Marcus leaned forward in his seat at the sound of tearing fabric. The woman was raking her nails through the seat. She turned around, searching for help, so Marcus stood up.

"Ma'am?" he said. He swayed in the aisle and tapped the woman's shoulder.

The woman cringed then bared her teeth, so Marcus withdrew.

Silence followed until the woman again scratched. Marcus listened and listened and finally understood. She was whispering curses.

They crashed down the block where vanilla gowns rattled automatic fire, and Marcus and everyone crackled three-round clusters. Sergeant Squirrel shouted and Marcus and Leroy dumped rounds until the mortar blasting ended and the street smoked violet. Cicadas shrilled in Marcus's ears. Footsteps padded through dust. He snaked third through the door and covered Leroy, but then came the wave of flames and, soundless, Leroy rammed his shoulder and outside they coughed. Between him and Leroy, the woman's mouth and eyes were open, and she wore black fabric slashed open where her stomach gaped.

Marcus awoke. That was what he'd remembered the morning in the dorm's weightroom, what had made Leroy pause when in danger. Now, since he was on a bus towards

Leroy's hometown, the question was whether Leroy hated him for it.

Near midnight, passengers boarded in Terre Haute. The woman who'd joined him in Richmond, who'd cursed a row in front, must have stepped from the bus in Indianapolis. He dozed off, finding himself on shore back home. Lake Erie lurched in frozen waves. Down the beach, a Siberian husky stared at him like an old man. Marcus scrambled to scale the breakwall, but the dog was bearing down.

Two days later, the bus arrived in Antiguo in the late afternoon. He inched down the center aisle with his backpack hunching him over and, the last one off, moved through the bus station lobby. The border city of Antiguo clustered, one story high brick and adobe buildings. Out front, the sun glared off concrete that lifted warm waves. Marcus at last found his friend. Leroy slumped in the passenger seat of a Chevy van, biting his thumbnail.

He called out, and Leroy spat the sliver and leaned with his ashen arm out the van window. He'd grown out his hair to hide the scar on his scalp.

"You look the same," Leroy said, and he pulverized Marcus's knuckles when they shook.

Marcus slid open the van door with smarting fingers, and in front of him sat a long-legged girl hugging a pink backpack.

"That's my sister Persia. She's fourteen," Leroy warned. Marcus closed the door, and the driver surged forward into traffic. "And this is my pop." Leroy had gotten his shoulders and neck from his father. Sitting behind them, Marcus felt like he'd come set behind two offensive guards.

At Leroy's house that evening, they feasted. Leroy's father sizzled ribs on the backyard grill while his mother picked up toys and wiped down surfaces with a rag and bleach. The living room served as a daycare center during the day.

Marcus guzzled beer with Leroy, who slouched in a wheelchair before the kitchen table. Sometimes the beer inspirited Leroy so that he flailed his arms in praise of the ribs ("Soaked in Colt 45," he said, "all night softening the meat") and, the next moment, he sank over his food as though brooding over some grievance. During Leroy's silence, his mother, Bessa, heaped greens and potatoes ("Another half-rack, Marcus?") onto his plate, and Leroy's father, Joe, asked about Cleveland. When he was sixteen, Joe had run away from home and stayed with an uncle there. He'd gotten a job working on the docks and, in '69, smoked cigarettes on the hood of a cousin's Chevy while watching the Cuyahoga River in flames.

After coffee that night, Bessa cleared the table, and Persia kissed her brother, her father, and even Marcus on the cheek before going to bed. Leroy's father ground the butt of his cigarette in the ashtray and stood from the table. He gripped Leroy around the shoulder and told Marcus he'd drop him off at the airport the next morning on his way to work.

"Don't stay up too late," Joe said and headed into the kitchen, where coffee cups clinked together in the sink.

Minutes later, Bessa dropped a pillow and a folded blanket on the living room couch for Marcus.

"You boys staying up much later?"

"Little while," Leroy said. "A coke, Marcus?"

Bessa went to bed, and Leroy wheeled himself into the kitchen. He brought back whiskey.

"Tight family," Marcus said.

Leroy dropped shot glasses onto the table, peeled the plastic off the bottleneck, and twisted open the cap. "They aight."

After he filled the glasses, he lifted his glass and tilted it towards Marcus.

"To being back," Leroy said, peering at the whiskey.

Marcus swallowed. Through the tears, Leroy seemed to be snarling at him, but he wasn't. He was opening and closing his hand and wincing.

"What's wrong?"

"Did something to my wrist whomping that sack of goddamn sand," Leroy said. He made a fist and squeezed, veins swelling under the skin. Leroy and Marcus, although they'd met at basic, had befriended each other in the ruined dorm outside Baghdad. Before night patrols or daytime guarding of fuel, Leroy had been notorious for whaling away at the punching bag, psyching the whole platoon up. Many marines had used it, but Leroy's bag routine had been unique. He'd never hit the bag with combos but instead would slam the bag with fifty left hooks, making it depress in the middle like a hanged man's mid-section, sometimes sending it into revolutions, until he stopped it by swiveling his hips to slam the bag with fifty hooks from his right. Since Marcus was the only other brother who used the weightroom before booting up, soon he was spotting the bag Leroy punished. Exhausted, Leroy would spin away from the bag, his shoulders and arms blasted, and howl like a devil dog. It righted everyone's mind.

It was eleven thirty. A wall clock ticked. After he again filled both glasses to the brim, Leroy leaned forward with his elbows on the table. The tattoo on his shoulder read, *Boot up or shut up.*

"Look like you been working out," Marcus said. "That how you hurt it again?"

"Nah," Leroy said. "They been fitting a leg to me and making me train." He clasped his hand around his glass. "Drink." He lifted the glass and this time peered at Marcus. "To getting better."

Marcus exhaled the fumes, unsure how much longer he could stand Leroy's mood. If this went on, he would get up and crash on the couch. "What about those cokes?" Marcus said.

"Got a email from buck-face." Leroy's head lolled to one side as he stared beyond Marcus.

"You mean Squirrel?" Marcus almost snickered, but Leroy was grinding his teeth.

"He knocked up Sheila." Leroy was slurring. "Man must think he better than us."

"But they married."

Leroy's nostrils flared. "Ain't what I meant, man." He paused, then continued, "Phil kids—three in a row born dead." He chopped his hand three times on the table. He raised the glass and tipped it to his lips, and Marcus downed his shot too. The room revolved. Out the window, black-purple splashed the sky.

"But Phil got there before us," Marcus said. Phil Michaels's unit had stormed into Baghdad during the bombardment, the contaminating dust Leroy blamed for Michael's luck at its heaviest.

"For oil," Leroy said, dragging the bottle towards him. (Marcus snorted at the overused phrase. *I didn't go for that*, he thought.) Leroy poured whiskey onto the table but finally found the glasses. "Someone getting rich off all this."

Marcus downed the whiskey. "What about what Squirrel said?"

Leroy drank and glared at Marcus until Marcus looked away.

"Same old Marcus," Leroy said through his teeth, but still he nudged Marcus's glass closer to slop whiskey into it. "Drink, nigga."

They drank, and Leroy squeezed the empty glass.

The plane glided over earth raked through with ditches before it sank into smog (even in the air, Marcus whiffed it), and the city surfaced as though from underground. Soon the plane touched down and docked, and outside the window, letters on the terminal announced, Aeropuerto Internacional de la Ciudad de México.

Marcus shouldered the backpack and left the plane. After he passed through the airport in a line of fellow foreigners, a custom's officer slammed a red stamp into his passport. Marcus tucked the book into his pocket and, after making his way through the baggage-claim floor (he only had the backpack), stepped through metal detectors. Doors slid open. He burrowed through a crowd of people holding signs with names on them. Their voices quieted as he hurried towards the main exit, where Oscar said he'd be waiting.

Taxi drivers barked outside while exhaust tingled his nostrils. In front of him stretched a line of taxis, and beyond them, city traffic churned past. The engines, all together, sounded like shovels breaking up the ground.

Marcus had spoken on the phone with Rosita first.

"I'm Marcus," he'd said. "My father is Samuel Green." He'd said he wanted to visit Oscar.

"Por qué?" Rosita had said.

Marcus had paused. "Because I'd nearly forgotten him."

Rosita and Marcus shared no blood, so what would he mean to her? The son of the other woman and nothing more? Most of what he knew about Rosita he'd heard from his mother. She'd told him before he'd taken the bus to Texas. "Your father got her pregnant in '77," his mother said as though outlining an argument, "the year he left the Peace Corps. We married in '81, you came along in '82, and four years later, that woman after all that time mails a letter announcing she has his child, even sends photos so it's clear the boy's his. When he took you and went, he was telling me he wasn't coming back, even though he did, but by then it was long done."

Rosita had replied by saying Oscar would be there the next time Marcus called. And Oscar was.

Marcus spoke with Oscar three days before boarding the bus to Texas.

"Do you remember," Marcus had asked, "playing mango baseball with the shovel?"

"No," Oscar had said, "but *Marcus* baseball, sí." Oscar's grainy voice had broken into a laugh.

Marcus rubbed the back of his head, remembering how Oscar had missed the mango and instead clanged the tool against his skull. He wished he had a more recent photo of Oscar. Anyway, he thought, it'll be easier for him to find me. He leaned back against the wall, the backpack between his feet, and waited. We will take the Pullman de Morelos, he thought, and visit Rosita.

Beside him, people shuffled up steps. He peeked around the corner. Two men turned the stairwell corner and surfaced from the underground terminal floor. The first man's gaunt face startled him. The sunken eyes turned up and met his, so Marcus jerked back and leaned against the wall. This first man wore a baseball cap and slouched, his baggy pants swishing as he strode towards the curb in front of Marcus to scan the street.

The second man to emerge had the build of a featherweight boxer. The gangly man at the curb nodded, and the boxer squared up in front of Marcus.

It was Oscar. A silver cross hung from his neck. The necklace tangled with other necklaces, one a circle under his Adam's apple that depicted the Virgin. Tattoos wholly blotted out the skin on his left arm, and a black tattoo, a dagger with a drop of red on the end, stabbed the skin of his neck. Marcus's burns seemed to trouble him, and Marcus realized why. *Oscar doesn't know I've been mutilated.*

"Hermano?" Marcus said. The man on the curb stared. He wore a sweatshirt with a hood on it and kept his hand in the shirt's front pocket.

Marcus held out his hand to shake. A calendar of some sort exploded around a sun on the back of Oscar's hand.

Oscar pivoted, his face smoothing out like a dazzled child's, and leapt forward, picking Marcus up in a bear hug. "Hermano!"

He dropped Marcus and snatched up his backpack. He wore his hair long on top and slicked back. With his tattooed hand, he punched Marcus on the shoulder and said, unbelieving, "Mi hermano." It was almost a question. His voice was raspy, the voice of a smoker. He gripped Marcus's shoulders. "Vámonos," he said, beaming, and ushered Marcus down the stairs.

"I'm looking forward to seeing your mother," Marcus said. He glanced back at the Pullman de Morelos buses they were leaving behind.

"We will," Oscar said. Sweat glazed his forehead, and he turned away from Marcus, hunching as if prepared to brawl. He led Marcus through travelers. What is he guarding for? Marcus thought. Oscar turned around and grinned, face reddening. On the back of his arm, a dragon whipped its tail. The dragon lurched from the wrist until, along the fat of the tricep, it snarled bearing jaws and talons.

They maneuvered through people, ran up another set of steps, and arrived beneath an overpass. The air smelled of exhaust.

"Aquí," Oscar said, and he and Marcus stood by the curb while cars swished by. Oscar, blushing, gripped Marcus's shoulder again and squeezed. He asked about the trip, so Marcus recounted it, moving back in time and location until in his mind he found himself in Ohio. All at once it seemed pitiful that, although he had come, their father had stayed away.

The skinny man lagged and leaned in a corner by a pillar to light a cigarette. He smoked with one hand in his pocket, his baseball cap low over his eyes.

"Don't worry about Delgado," Oscar said. "He lived in Los Angeles for three years." Oscar shrugged as though Marcus should understand.

"What happened?"

"They were always fighting," Oscar said and rubbed his hand over his tattooed arm, "*con negros*." He then bounced, shaking out his arms, as though loosening himself up for a fight. "Here comes our ride."

An economy Nissan car swerved towards them and stopped. Two men sat inside. Delgado flicked the cigarette away and hunched forward, slipping first into the back seat. Marcus climbed in second, and Oscar scooted in last and shut the door. He held Marcus's backpack on his lap.

"Meet my brother, cabrónes," Oscar said.

The driver was Carlos, who smiled tenderly at Marcus. Carlos had a baby face when he grinned, but he gripped the wheel with both bony-knuckled hands and sweated, pale, when he drove. The man in the passenger seat was Hugo. The wrinkles of skin beneath his eyes made him look forty, but Hugo had hard strips of muscle on either side of the jaw and, Marcus thought, must've been an athlete. Hugo regarded Marcus as though Marcus were a wall.

"We're brothers," the driver, Carlos, said. He leaned forward and smiled in the rearview mirror. "Hugo, Delgado, and I are brothers *por sangre*, and Oscar for what we've done together. Por lo que hemos hecho juntos, verdad, Oscar?"

Oscar slapped Marcus's shoulder. "Now you're with us."

Carlos's eyes turned on Marcus in the mirror, and Hugo twisted around in the passenger seat. "You like being our brother?" Hugo said.

"Of course," Marcus said. "That's why I've come."

Hugo gazed, blank. "You were a soldado?"

"A marine."

"Kill Iraqis?" Carlos asked, smiling with beetling incisors. His baby face reddened, but then he sat up straight and lifted his chin. "Delgado here was in the Mexican Army," Carlos said, "but now he's our soldado."

Delgado glared. His cheekbones bulged.

"You like México?" Hugo said.

"We're going to show you México," Carlos said. Both his hands clasped the wheel. "We need to do something first." They slowed for a stoplight. Carlos hung his arm out the window and leaned towards the rearview mirror. "Or Delgado's got to do something."

Oscar brushed his fingers over the tattooed forearm.

"We're family," Hugo said. "You like our family?"

"I do," Marcus said. He turned towards Oscar. "How's your mother?"

"We're going to show you *México*," Carlos said. "Forget about his mother."

"She's well," Oscar said. Carlos's eyes held steady in the rearview mirror.

They stopped at a streetlight. A semi idled beside them, and between the cars walked a man pulling candy from a paper bag and shouting. Far ahead, a silver skyscraper with a long needle thrust into the sky.

"Marcus," Carlos said, "why are you serious?"

Hugo wrenched around in the seat. Delgado shifted.

"No," Marcus said. "Hung over."

Carlos drove on, traffic all around them. "Oscar's also serious," Carlos said as a general announcement. "Why so serious, güey?"

"I'm emotional," Oscar said, "because a brother's materialized from nowhere."

"Too shocked to go with Delgado," Carlos said mournfully.

The main square opened up in front of them, and Carlos crept the car around it. The square spread flat, inlaid with earth-gray tiles of stone. Government buildings with facades like forts and crimson window awnings surrounded a tremendous flapping flag.

"No," Oscar said, "I'll go with Delgado."

"Hugo will go," Carlos said, "and you'll entertain your brother."

"Delgado's my brother, güey."

Carlos stopped the car. "We'll show you México when we get back," Carlos said.

Oscar flung open the door, and as soon as Marcus stepped out, Carlos sped off.

Oscar faced the flag in the middle of the square. The sky was white behind it.

"I'm sorry," Marcus said. "A friend got me drunk last night."

Oscar turned, smiling. "Don't worry," he said. He bumped his fist against Marcus's shoulder. "There's nothing to worry about."

They walked from the plaza and down a street of vendors. Behind the vendors were shops and restaurants, and above, towels, shirts, and jeans dangled from apartment windows. Marcus leaned forward to bear the backpack. Oscar turned into an open restaurant, the entrance resembling an open garage in Ohio. A cook at a long grill stirred beef mixed with onions and diced green peppers. A chunk of beef beside the cook spun on a stake.

"Buen día," the cook said when they entered, and with a butcher knife, he sliced slivers of meat off the spinning hunk.

Oscar walked to a table in the rear of the room. The table was plastic and round, and Oscar slipped into a chair with his back facing a corner. Marcus recognized why: Oscar was guarding his rear and flanks. *Why?* In spite of Oscar's smiles and raspy confidentiality, Marcus felt like he had in Baghdad, with his mind casting outward to surrounding blocks, wary of his intrusion. His unit's enemies back there had been residents, so Marcus had marched or ridden in convoys through the Al-Salaam district feeling, by comparison, lost. Now he slid the backpack off his shoulder and pulled out a chair. The plastic legs grated over the cement, and he eased himself down. They were the only ones eating.

A girl asked Marcus and Oscar what they wanted to drink, and after they'd ordered beer, Marcus asked what Carlos and the boys were doing.

"Getting paid," Oscar said and ran his index finger down his menu.

"Doing what?"

"Many things."

The girl brought their beer bottles and clinked two drinking glasses onto the table. She'd run a slice of lime over the rim of each glass before dipping it in salt. When Marcus drank, salt clung to the corners of his mouth. He licked it away and crunched. The waitress took from the tray three black bowls and placed them on the table. Each bowl held a kind of salsa. After she tucked the tray under her armpit, she asked Marcus what he wanted, and he said he'd have whatever his brother ordered. Oscar said barbacoa.

Oscar leaned back in his chair, interlocking his fingers behind his head, and gazed up at a mounted television. A soccer game was showing. He chewed the pink of his bottom lip and flared his nostrils.

The waitress brought a tray with two steaming plates that she placed before them. Provolone cheese melted like netting over a mound of crispy, grilled beef, and green pepper and diced onion glistened, still sizzling. The waitress laid in front of Marcus and Oscar baskets that held towels. Oscar dumped red salsa over the beef and, with a fork poised in one hand, flipped open a towel's corner. He swiped a soft tortilla from the basket, rolled it up, and held it in one hand. Then he shoveled stringy beef into his mouth with a fork, biting into the tortilla between forkfuls.

"I haven't eaten all day," Oscar said, hunched forward.

"It's good," Marcus said. "Do you live here?" He dumped a spoonful of green salsa on his beef. He remembered chickens outside Oscar's house, below the palm trees outside the kitchen window.

"Sometimes."

"Sometimes you live in Cuernavaca? With your mother?" The salsa felt cool on his palate, but then it burned. He fumbled for the beer.

"No, I stay with my aunt and uncle. My mother and her hombre moved out. You'll see the farm tomorrow."

"I'd almost forgotten about the farm, but I remember the trees."

"The ahuehuetes are still in the middle of the field. Nobody's cut them."

"What are they?"

"Árboles. If you remember trees, you probably remember those." Oscar leaned over the table and lifted Marcus's empty glass. He then whistled to get the waitress's attention. "Dos más," he said. The light from the street paled Oscar's face, and his eyes reflected passing cars and people. Outside the shop, cars moved by and voices echoed. Oscar lifted his glass and spun it, swirling the last swallow at the glass's bottom. Lime seeds floated. Finally Oscar inhaled and sat erect, awakening from his daydream. The beer had come, so he drank the rest of his old one. "My brother's here," Oscar said. He faced straight ahead when he lifted the glass and clinked it against Marcus's.

After they ate and paid, Oscar held his hands in fists as they reentered the streets. They returned to the central plaza that government buildings surrounded, radio needles jutting from roofs alongside flagpoles. Three teenagers sat on the ground, legs crossed, passing around a joint. One of them murmured something about Americans. Marcus stood shoulder-to-shoulder with his brother, the sky dim and formless.

"Here," Oscar said, and the Nissan flew towards them around the square.

Delgado scooted over and let them in. Marcus sat in the middle, Oscar by the door.

"Cómo fue?" Oscar said.

"No sé," Carlos said. He hit the gas pedal.

A smell Marcus recognized lingered, bitter and heavy. Beside him, Delgado's right hand trembled. He wore only a wife-beater, his hooded sweatshirt stuffed in front of him on his feet. Across his belly, red-orange smeared the white shirt.

Carlos, both hands on the wheel, drove through city streets. Vending tables, pedestrians, and fenced off cathedrals blurred by. All the car windows were open, so exhaust-bittered air gusted violently over Marcus's face.

At five in the morning, Marcus collapsed drunk on the floor of the brothers' apartment in Mexico City, and the next afternoon, he and Oscar stumbled to the Pullman de Morelos station. Marcus at last would visit Rosita and Oscar.

In Cuernavaca, they boarded an intracity bus, *una ruta*, and stepped off in the village of Progreso. White clouds hid the sun. They walked along a dirt road flanked by a wall, a place Marcus found familiar. Hillside villages surrounded them, and Marcus smelled manure. Hay and wheat fields had bristled along the road during the bus ride. What else did they farm here? They walked along the mud-packed wall, and a smell of flowers wafted over it.

"This is my aunt and uncle's farm now," Oscar said, "not my madre's anymore."

Oscar waved Marcus towards the wall and pointed up. Glass bottle bottoms jutted from the top, functioning like razor wire.

"Mira," Oscar said, and he stepped forward, spread out his legs for balance, and interlocked his fingers. Marcus took hold of a stone in the wall and stepped up into his brother's hands.

Over the edge lolled fields of roses. They spread for acres. A breeze blew and made the flowers nod. So this, he thought, was where I came with Dad. He lifted his face to the scent before he tired and dropped.

"That's where the party's at," Oscar said.

(The night before, Oscar and the brothers had taken Marcus to a bar. The bar had one back wall, the rest open to the air. They'd slouched around a table, ordering beer, pan-fried fish, and, Marcus soon realized, women.

"Say it, Marcus," Carlos had said while hefting a glass of beer before him. Salt frosted the rim of everyone's glass, and lime juice swirled heavy at the bottom. Everyone lifted his beer and leaned forward, watching Marcus.

"*A güevo!*" Marcus said as ordered and gulped down a mouthful. Oscar and the brothers wailed in laughter while the girl Carlos had paid to snuggle against Marcus tittered. Her eyes were bloodshot, and she'd gelled her yellow-brown hair slantwise over her face to hide infected fingernail scratches. After midnight, Carlos had ordered a round of tequila shots because Cinco de Mayo had just begun.)

Now, Marcus followed Oscar along the wall. They turned a corner and came to a gate. Oscar tugged a rope that jingled bells. At last, Marcus thought, I will meet Rosita.

The gate stretched across the opening of an earthen trail. The trail curved off and disappeared behind an outbuilding. Ahead, through low-hanging branches, stood the pale side of a two-story adobe farmhouse. Laughter echoed off the flat surface.

A boy's feet pattered down the trail towards them. The boy stopped and stared at Oscar's arm.

"Jesús," Oscar said, "it's me."

The boy Jesús wore dirt-smudged tennis shoes with slacks, and his dress shirt collar hung open. He turned back down the trail and shouted. "Es Oscar!"

Jesús unlocked the chain on the gate and looked at Oscar's tattoos. The three of them started down the trail towards the laughter, ducking under leaves. The smell of the rose fields swept over them.

Jesús peeked at Marcus from the other side of Oscar, and Oscar gripped the silver cross over his chest.

("Why so many necklaces?" Marcus had asked, tequila burning his throat.

"Porque," Carlos said. A shot glass was suspended in his fingers. "Saints saved his life."

Oscar yanked up his shirt and showed where a bullet had slipped into his guts and blown out his back.

"And that one?" Marcus asked, meaning the scar that raked across his navel.

"That?" Oscar said. "We all have one."

The brothers lifted their shirts. They all bore matching knife blade gashes.)

Nearing the end of the trail, Oscar kissed the cross. The tree leaves brought out the green of his eyes and rustled.

In a clearing, people holding beers lounged around a table. Children, two girls and a boy, ran and lifted dust. The two girls scampered away and climbed onto the lap of a woman, who sat at the head of the table and wore a straw hat. A long weave hung over her shoulder and almost brushed the ground. A crimson ribbon tightened around the tip of the weave.

It's Rosita, and she's as youthful now as when Dad snapped those photos.

Jesús broke off from Marcus's group and scooped the little boy up. Unlike the girls, the boy had swayed dumbstruck when Marcus and Oscar had emerged from the trees. Jesús lugged the boy over to the woman laden with watchful children.

A young, black-haired girl leaned forward beside Rosita. A paintbrush dangled between her fingers. Scarlet paint loaded the end of the brush, and a ceramic pot glistened shiny brown on the table before her. She resembled Rosita. It must be Rosita's daughter, he thought, from a man other than Dad. Beyond the table, the rose fields rippled.

Marcus opened his mouth to speak, but the woman blushed and stroked the head of a girl in her lap. Marcus hesitated. Beside him, three other people stared as if bewildered. One was a young man with a balding head of hair slicked back, and beside him was a middle-aged man with a black t-shirt and sunglasses. The other person at the table was a woman whose shortly cropped silver hair feathered back to muffle her ears. She sat upright, hands pressed together and clamped between her knees.

"Mama," Oscar said as though it was an apology. He tucked the tattooed arm behind him and dropped his head.

The youthful woman with the children stared across the table, and the somber woman with silver hair, the woman near Marcus, tilted her head. Oscar, eyelids shut as though grieving, knelt and pressed his lips to this woman's cheekbone. He rested his forehead on his mother's shoulder. The cross on Oscar's neck dropped against her arm. "My brother's come back, Mama," Oscar said.

The woman turned her silver head, and Marcus stepped forward. She regarded him, her mouth lifeless. The woman across the table, then, was Oscar's aunt. *This* was Rosita.

Marcus leaned over and kissed her cheek, and Rosita groaned.

Oscar nodded sharply at the man in black sunglasses. "Gustavo," Oscar said, but Gustavo swigged from a bottle.

"Marcus," Oscar said, squeezing the shoulder of the next person over, "this hombre here is my brother, like you." The balding younger man had a scar beneath his eye. "Pepe's a police officer." Pepe smirked and reached out to shake hands with Marcus. He had Gustavo's pitbull jaws and must have been the son of Gustavo and Rosita. Gustavo peered through the glasses and ignored Oscar.

Oscar then introduced Marcus to his aunt, Lulú, and to all her children. He'd already met Jesús, and the three little ones were Edgar, Maria, and Sucena. The girl who'd been dabbing paint onto the ceramic pot was Lulú's older daughter Amora. She had sleek hands no wider than her wrists, and her black hair fell straight and sharp over her shoulders and below the seat of her chair. When she rose to make room for Marcus and Oscar, the hair fell past her hips. She stood a foot shorter than Oscar and wore a red, light summer dress.

"Cervezas?" Amora said. Red paint smudged her brow.

"Dos," Oscar said, and he lunged forward to capture Amora in his arms. Amora screamed as Oscar kissed her cheek. "No," Oscar said, tilting Amora away from Marcus, "you can't kiss my cousin."

The children around the table giggled, Marcus beamed, and Amora wiped Oscar's slobber off her face with the back of her hand. Blushing, she hurried into a cinderblock outbuilding. Wisps of hair brushed against her hips.

After nightfall, Oscar's half-brother Pepe brought out a piñata for Cinco de Mayo. The children squealed to swing first. The piñata dangled from the end of a rope Pepe had slung over a tree branch.

"Youngest first," Pepe said, so Lulú's two little girls first tried to beat open the ceramic bear, but the stick only tapped the piñata. Pepe tugged the rope, and the bear escaped some of the girls' swings.

After Edgar whacked the bear without breaking it, Pepe handed Jesús the stick. Jesús shuffled forward until his mother Lulú shouted. She blindfolded him for fairness, and the three younger children surrounded him as he twirled the stick over his head.

"Da-le, da-le, da-le," the children sang, "no pierdas el tino ... porque si lo pierdes, pierdes el camino..."

"Did you take advantage of Mexico City last night?" Gustavo said, the first words he'd directed to Marcus, almost three hours after Marcus had sat down.

"We expected you last night," Rosita said. Oscar had dragged his chair next to his mother. He was holding her yellowish hand.

Gustavo nudged away empty beer bottles and flipped through a stack of photographs. He held a photo out for Marcus. Marcus took it, and Gustavo jabbed his thumb towards his son Pepe, who tugged the rope. In the photo, Pepe wore a police uniform and aimed a pistol with both hands at an enemy outside the photograph.

"Hit the piñata," the children sang, *"but don't break the load..."*

Gustavo snatched back the photo. He looked at it before replacing it on the stack. "Did you meet Oscar's friends?" Gustavo said.

"...because if you break it, you'll break the road..."

"Gustavo needs another beer," Oscar said and elbowed Marcus. He lifted his own beer to his mouth and sipped.

"Sí, Tío?" Amora said. Amora drank Jamaica water, reddish-purple water flavored with flower petals. Marcus, sitting beside her, had sipped the sweet drink from her glass.

"No," Rosita said.

Gustavo downed his beer and thumped the bottle on the table. "Come on," he said. "Between these two boys, we've got a special American guest."

Pepe tugged the rope with both hands. Jesús cracked the bear in the belly and beat candy loose.

"Not again," Rosita said. She shook her bony finger at Amora. "We'll leave first."

"...you just hit it once, and just hit it again. You just hit it three times..."

"Oscar," Gustavo said, "don't those necklaces burn your skin?" Gustavo, eyes bloodshot, turned towards Marcus. He leaned forward with his arms on the table. "Is that what happened to you, Marcus?" Gustavo pronounced Marcus's name, *Marr-coose.*

"Father," Pepe said, "come here and help." As Pepe shouted, he held the piñata steady long enough for Jesús to strike. The stick broke open the bear's stomach. The bear's bottom half lay broken on the ground while the children roughhoused for candy.

"What *do* you do?" Gustavo said, pointing at Oscar.

Oscar's nostrils were flaring even though he smiled. "I try to stay alive, old man." He kneaded his mother's hand with both of his.

"We're leaving," Rosita said. Oscar's aunt Lulú rose from her chair.

"Mama," Oscar said, "let Gustavo go."

"Children," Oscar's aunt Lulú called, "inside for baths." The children pleaded with candy in their mouths.

Rosita pushed back the chair and sniffled while Gustavo swayed down the trail. Oscar scooted back the chair and tripped towards his mother. In front of her, he dropped his head and mumbled. Oscar threw his arms around his mother's shoulders.

"You stink like hell," Rosita said while hugging him.

"Adiós, Marcus," Rosita said before she turned down the trail and blended into the trees.

"Amora," Lulú said, holding the two little girls in her arms, "prepare the cots."

"Are you staying the night?" Jesús said. He had a lump of candy in his cheek and stared at Marcus's scarred arm.

Oscar hooked his hand on Marcus's shoulder and swayed. "Otra cerveza, hermano?"

Marcus fell against Oscar. "A güevo," Marcus said.

Amora walked towards the cinderblock outbuilding and swept aside the curtain in the doorway. *A wonderful, wonderful walk*, Marcus decided as he and Oscar followed, leaning against one another.

The outbuilding smelled like a basement. Darkness shifted in the room until Amora switched on a light. Marcus's hand shot up to block his eyes. Amora stood in front of the light and glowed golden.

"An angel," Marcus said. He tripped back onto one of the cots. On the wall beside him, a pair of shears hung on a nail.

Oscar plopped down on an overturned bucket. "I guess she isn't *your* cousin," he said.

Amora held her hand over her mouth and stepped towards the door.

"Leaving without kisses?" Oscar said. He stretched out his arms and legs, puckering his lips. He kicked over a shovel that clanged on the ground.

"Sí," Amora said over her shoulder and escaped.

Marcus got up and replaced the shovel against the wall.

"What's Amora do?" he said, taking beer bottles from the refrigerator and then handing one to Oscar.

"Goes to the state university." Oscar opened the beer. "Studies art, knows things about aesthetic law."

Marcus sat down, the cot creaking under his weight. He twisted off the beer cap and drank. "Your mother wasn't happy to see me," he said.

Oscar chugged from the bottle. "She's sick. Gustavo and Pepe take care of her." Oscar scratched the tattooed arm. "Wish I could, but Gustavo moved her off the farm."

Marcus drank from the bottle, leaning forward with his elbows on his knees. He wanted to ask Oscar what he knew or remembered about his father's being in that village for half a decade, but bells at the end of the trail jingled, and Oscar stood up. Oscar drank down the rest of his beer and staggered towards the door. He was leaning his shoulder against the doorframe when Carlos bawled his name from the gate.

"I'm going," Oscar said and turned off the light. "Sleep."

"When will you be back?"

"Don't worry," Oscar said, "be back soon." He swished the curtain back over the door, and his boots crunched down the trail. At the gate, Carlos whistled and laughed. Car doors shut, and the Nissan sputtered off.

The wind strengthened, and unfamiliar insects ticked in rhythmic waves. A breeze whipped in, covering him with a cool blanket.

Marcus neared sleep but heard footsteps in the dusty ground. He lifted his head from the pillow.

"Who's there?"

Wind puffed up the curtain over the door, shaping a breast, shoulder, arm, and hip, the contours of a woman.

CHAPTER 3

The next morning, Marcus slung a jug of iced Jamaica water over his shoulder and followed Jesús through the rose fields. Jesús lugged along a shovel, and straw hats haloed their heads as they moved out. Color organized the flowers, from yellow to pink to red, as the ground sloped away, and in the middle of the field rustled a cluster of immense trees whose leaves spiraled from ash-white limbs.

Jesús turned down a row of yellow flowers, and spreading his legs for balance, he thrust the shovel into the ground to uproot a clump of wildflowers. He continued down the row, digging up weeds, and once he'd finished, he dropped the shovel and walked under a tree. He kicked a basket overflowing with weeds, and a field snake slithered out and into an irrigation ditch. Jesús dumped the weeds and shyly handed the basket to Marcus.

"Help me?" he said. Once again, Jesús resembled Oscar from the photos.

That morning, Amora and Jesús had delivered breakfast to the outbuilding. Amora had brought a glass of milk and a plate of eggs. The eggs had been scrambled and mixed with shreds of tortilla. Jesús had carried another plate, with toast and a spoonful of pepper sauce.

"Where's Oscar?" Amora had said, handing Marcus the plate of eggs.

Marcus had blinked, trying to focus on Jesús. "Right there," he'd said.

Amora and Jesús had laughed. "Crudo," she'd said. *Hung over.*

Marcus dropped the jug at the base of the tree and returned to the fields. Jesús went back down a row of flowers, and Marcus dragged the basket down the first row to toss in the uprooted weeds. He cleaned the row and headed back down to unload and catch up with the boy, but he stopped half way because Jesús had missed a cluster of wildflowers. Marcus knelt and took hold. He yanked the weeds but also uprooted the bush, and the weeds' fine blades sliced his fingers. After the pain in his hand had stopped, he stamped the wild growth back down.

A half hour later, Jesús met Marcus by the waste heap under the tree and flung down the shovel. "Water," he said, dramatically hoarse, and lifted the canteen to his lips. He exhaled, satisfied, and pointed into the tree at mangos. "Quieres?" he said and took up the shovel. With a swat, he batted down a group and underhand tossed one to Marcus. They peeled their snacks, and sour green rind wedged under their fingernails. Marcus suspended the fruit over his mouth and squeezed juice onto his tongue.

Jesús again lifted the shovel and started in on another row. Marcus picked up a second fallen mango, peeled off the rind, and drank the juice. Afterwards he took up the jug of Jamaica water, ice cubes rattling, and chugged several mouthfuls.

Mountains all around him waved with swishing trees, and behind him, ivy decorated the roadside wall. There, a slightly bowlegged man, a straw hat slantwise on his head, was walking by. His round face turned towards Marcus, and his lips parted as though he wanted to ask something, but after a pause, the man moved on.

A skinny dog with the frame of a husky and the markings of a Rottweiler sniffed at the ground behind the man. The dog's nipples sagged, and the man's boots fell softly in the grass as he walked along the irrigation ditch, perhaps checking for blockage. Then he turned into the cluster of trees in the middle of the field and was gone. Marcus had almost returned to gathering weeds when a puppy whined behind him. The puppy sniffed his boot and licked the toe. It was black and tan like the dog he'd seen.

"Where'd you come from, little guy?" he said, kneeling. He ran his hand over its back and felt every bump of its spinal column. Its ribs protruded as if it was starving, so he slid his hand under its belly (surprisingly plump, perhaps it was all right) and chased after the man who'd just passed.

All the trees over the acres of farmland grew mangled from dusty earth, but this cluster formed an evergreen canopy. Marcus now realized they were cypress trees, the ahuehuetes Oscar had mentioned two days earlier. The leaves twisted at the base and wound down, helical. As soon as he entered the patch, the ground angled downward, and from ahead came the sound of trickling water. The puppy sniffed around, limp in his hand as he walked along the softened earth. He approached a creekside clearing.

Whoever the man was, he seemed to be living in a cinderblock shed smaller than the outbuilding Marcus was staying in. Bricks held the corrugated metal roof in place, and above the dwelling, the cypress trees opened up. Clouds still shifted, whitening the sky. The door of the shack was open, and inside, a desk stood against the wall by a bed, and books and papers covered it. In an earthen groove at the door of the shack, the pup's mother lay on its side.

The peasant crouched before the stream and dipped his hands in the water, then rubbed his eyes. Is this how the Russian vagrant, who'd lived in the shack behind his grandfather's house ninety years earlier, had lived? The man stood and gazed upstream.

While at first the patch of trees had mystified him, Marcus now realized its function. The rustling trees created a sundial that shaded the two main stretches of field, and like the trees around the fields back home, they probably enriched and retained moisture in the soil. It was something his father had taught him.

The puppy squirmed, so Marcus knelt and set it down, and it scrambled towards its mother.

Back at the farmhouse that evening, Jesús walked barefoot and shirtless from behind a plastic curtain that hung from a ring high above a drain, beside where a sink jutted from the outbuilding. He threw a towel to Marcus, and Marcus stepped behind the curtain and onto the wet cement. He used a bowl to scoop water from an open cistern and poured the water over his body. Chickens fluttered in a pen, and a goat baaed. Marcus lathered shampoo into his hair and rinsed with the refreshing water, and after drying, he slipped on pants and swiped aside the curtain. The goat bleated again. Beyond the animal's pen littered with corncobs, the sun was sinking.

He tiptoed barefoot across the ground and into the outbuilding. By the time he'd dressed, Jesús was calling. They walked through the cooler air of the trail, trees on both sides of them, and out the gate. They would walk along the wall, as Marcus had done the day before with Oscar, and take the bus to the central square of Cuernavaca.

At the Zócalo, they shouldered through street vendors and strolled along the Palace of Cortes. Soon they approached music and the smell of steamed vegetables and sizzling beef. In a newspaper stand, dozens of papers hung from metal clips. One front page showed photos from a murder in Mexico City. Masked gunmen, the headline read, machine-gunned a businessman's car yesterday. The photos showed the man's three children still belted in the back seat of the family car. Bullets had punctured their chests. Another newspaper showed insurgents sprawled across a stretch of road in An Najaf.

Beside the palace, Marcus and Jesús walked under a canopy of tarps and through covered vending tables. White-clothed tables displayed silver while other tables held wooden animals and paintings.

"My sister," Jesús said.

Sunlight from an opening in the tarps showered Amora. She rested her elbows on the table, a strand of hair clinging to her lip. She painted a vase, and her toes meshed around the foot bar. She had muscular calves and ankles.

Jesús dashed forward and made Amora gasp. He wrapped his arms around her waist, pushing the dress up so that her knees showed under the boy's arms. As Marcus approached, Amora pushed Jesús away and drew the dress down.

"Mamá," Jesús called, and Lulú, youthful, hospitable, like Rosita from the photos, hummed something at the next table. Jesús grasped his mother's thigh and tightened the dress around her flesh. Jesús then lifted one of his little sisters and kissed her stomach.

"Are you enjoying your visit?" Amora said. She swished the paintbrush in a cup of water.

"Your family has taken good care of me," he said, "except your brother. He had me working the fields today."

"He told Mamá last night he wanted a tattoo." She dipped the brush into paint. "He needs his father."

"Where is your father?"

"Working in Texas. He returns every December thirsty for México."

"The farm provides México beautifully," Marcus said. He fondled a ring on Amora's table. After realizing it featured the sunburst, he snatched it up.

"El dios del sol," she said. "Does it suit you?"

The sun god intoned, solemn and awful, at the center of the sharp-edged, metallic sun. It was the same design tattooed on Oscar's hand.

"I also have paintings," she said.

Marcus fingered a stack of moist paper. The sun god ordered seasons in bold yellow, green, orange, and red.

"These are yours?" he said. Amora said they were, so Marcus pulled a painting from the stack and held it out. The two-dimensional image was, somehow, both alarming and comforting. He handed Amora the painting and said he'd buy it.

"Have you visited Teotihuacán?" she said. "The necropolis?"

"I don't think so."

"The Aztec gave this god a pyramid." She rolled the painting up and fastened it with twine.

"Is it your god?"

Amora laughed. "No."

"Then why paint it so much?"

"The pattern pleases me," she said. "Its form is its function."

"A calendar."

"Sí, and nothing so necessary is made in vain. There's a filament of godliness in it."

The marketplace was shutting down, so she handed him the painting and stuffed blankets into a basket. Lulú gathered wares together, wrapping vases in paintings, paintings in blankets. The three younger children watched Marcus, and Jesús sipped water from a cup.

"Let me help," he said.

Amora hooked a basket on each of his arms, and when they'd packed up, with even the little ones holding a vase or bundle of blankets, they all walked from the marketplace.

At the bottom of the palace stairs, they boarded a bus. Marcus placed the goods in the aisle and squeezed between Jesús and Amora in the back row. Amora's body smelled sharp, like a blanket worn all night beside a campfire. A wisp of her hair tickled his arm.

"I want to go," he said, "to the pyramid."

"Bueno," she said and cast her eyes downward.

After Marcus placed the goods in the farmhouse kitchen, Amora asked if he'd like to walk to the village center.

"An hour," Lulú said. "I'll have dinner by then."

So Amora and Marcus walked back down the walled street, and Jesús followed.

"I saw a man today," Marcus said, "who lives in the trees by the stream."

Amora blushed. "Es my uncle."

"What's he do?"

"He calls himself a philosopher," she said, "but he's a hermit until he gets a book out."

At the village center, they walked along a wall of storefronts and homes before buying ice cream at a corner shop. In the square, smooth cement benches surrounded a raised gazebo, and roses sprouted from flowerbeds around the gazebo base.

Children chased a soccer ball under streetlights. Jesús sprinted to join them. Some knew Jesús by name and added him to the match without changing the flow of action.

"Do you see Oscar much?" Marcus said.

"More often since you called," she said. "Before that, it was as if he'd gone *por siempre*."

The children hollered while playing the match, and Marcus gasped when two dogs darted around the gazebo legs. A larger spaniel chased a mutt, both dogs jumping on and off benches. The mutt crashed into Marcus's stomach and muddied his lap. It twirled around, knocked the ice cream from his hand, and leapt away, the spaniel nipping its tail.

Children burst into laughter. Everyone on the playground had seen the spectacle, but the next moment, a boy took advantage of a weakened defense by launching the ball the length of the court, almost scoring a goal. The match restarted.

Amora laughed and covered her mouth with her hand. Vanilla dripped down her knuckles, so she licked it, and Marcus wondered if what he felt then was the feeling that had made his father stay five years. At least on that night, with Amora beside him and the children running, he felt himself within a harmonized pattern. If his father had also felt this way, why had he left? Had his work here, perhaps, injured someone?

"In your art," he said, "is there always the filament you talked about?"

"You mean the sun god?" She licked at her ice cream again. "No, sometimes it disturbs me. I don't know why. I meant that image wastes nothing, has wholeness."

"My father, do you know what he did here?"

Amora turned to him. "Don't you?"

"Nobody ever told me."

"My mother knows," she said and, sliding her hand over his thigh, crunched on the cone.

CHAPTER 4

Marcus, Amora, and Jesús walked back to the farmhouse amid flower fields. The moon shimmered, an amber womb. Something swelled inside (like in last night's dream, when the spider with the bulbous abdomen devoured an inchworm, and the worm, visible inside the spider's belly, grew into an asp). It soared above Marcus while he touched Amora, and Jesús turned up his face, aware something had changed. Holding Amora's hand, Marcus made the boy blush, but Jesús strolled beside his sister and the American stranger, his arms swinging out at his sides, and the moon pulsated behind Marcus in the sable sky.

In Antiguo, how was Leroy doing? Marcus's face burned, itched. He wondered how deep Leroy's anger still ran—deeper, perhaps, than Leroy himself could fully understand or articulate. Marcus wanted to be forgiven. He ought to be able to walk like this, with Amora beside him, holding her hand in scented air. He wasn't hiding from anything.

At the farmhouse gate, Marcus felt aroused when Amora's hand touched the hard muscle around his navel. This brought forth unwanted images—Kia reaching from her window, the black-gowned woman slouching among trees. Was it this type of memory, from his father's life, that had made his father return to Ohio?

Jesús latched the gate behind them, and Amora stepped in front of Marcus and halted. He collided with her backside and gripped her hips. The thin summer dress was slippery over her skin. Amora turned and, her hands pressing over Marcus's hands, shouted back to Jesús.

"The light, Papí," she said, and the light switch clicked, a canopy of black fell over them, and Amora pushed out her hips, rubbed Marcus's hands over her breasts, and, gasping, bent in his arms to offer her mouth. The rustling trees sounded like Lake Erie's waves. Jesús ran through the dark, and Amora broke free and strode away.

Marcus and Jesús rose last from the dinner table. Lulú and Amora had taken plates into the kitchen, and the three smaller children raced into the living room and sprawled over the couch and floor to watch television. Lulú wrapped plastic over bowls that held leftovers and slid them into the refrigerator. She then asked Jesús to go with her to the cistern outside, and Jesús groaned. Lugging water into the house for baths was heavy work.

Marcus leaned against a counter in the kitchen, again alone with Amora. She smiled, walking towards him, and wrapped her arms around his waist. Her forehead lingered in front of his mouth. She fastened an apron around him. Her head smelled sweaty.

At the sink, he lathered soapsuds over cups, silverware, plates, and bowls while Amora rinsed and arranged the dishes on a rack. Periodically Jesús and his mother entered with dripping buckets of water and poured them into a pot before going back outside.

With his hands pruned and sensitive, Marcus followed Amora towards the stairs that led to her upstairs room. She lifted one leg onto a step, and Marcus pushed up behind her. He sniffed the thin fabric of her dress, inhaled her body scent, but she twisted around (a hip against his stomach) and prodded his chest with her fingers.

"After I bring you breakfast," she said, "we'll go to Teotihuacán."

She meant the Aztec necropolis, but his hands cupped her hips, and he caressed the skin of her inner-thigh. Amora's eyelids sagged, and her arm slackened. She blushed, nudging him away, then whisked up the steps towards an exposed bulb that showered her with light.

A fragrant breeze flowed through the door and over the room when Jesús and Lulú hauled buckets of water through the front door, into the kitchen. Amora's door closed upstairs, so Marcus walked back into the dining room. He stopped in the kitchen entryway. Jesús was pouring water into the pot, and Lulú adjusted a dial on the oven to sterilize the bathwater. Jesús brushed past Marcus and joined the other children in front of the television.

Lulú's face glistened, her cheeks ruddy.

"I'm beginning to understand why my father stayed so long."

91

She wiped the counter, her whole body giving leverage. The weave of hair fell rhythmically against her buttocks.

Marcus stepped into the kitchen, and Lulú lifted her hand to her chest. With his wounded face suddenly close, he seemed to have alarmed her. "Lulú, what did my father do here?"

She opened her hand as though flinging seed and looked around. "All this," she said. Her lips pressed tightly together. "He made this place."

"Made it how?"

"My sister knows more," she said. "Why don't you ask her?"

"You mean he built this farmhouse?"

"He was part of a team. I don't know all they did. Vaccinated cows, I think, and marked which trees shouldn't be cut."

"But why'd he leave? What did he do wrong?"

"Rosita knows more," she said, "but even if I knew, it wouldn't make sense anymore."

After saying goodnight to Lulú, he left the farmhouse. His boots crunched over the ground as he approached the outbuilding. He swept aside the curtain over the doorway and, groping in the darkness, found the switch.

Marcus woke to sounds of someone walking down the trail. Further away, the stream babbled through the cypress trees, and overhead, moths battered the light bulb he'd left on. The footsteps grew louder until someone swept aside the curtain.

It had only been one day, but the skin around Oscar's eyes had blackened, and his face looked thinner. "Still up?" Oscar asked.

Oscar said he and the boys had to go away to Chiapas for a few days. During his absence, Marcus would be flying back to Texas, so Oscar had come to take Marcus out one final night. Too groggy to argue (was Oscar leaving him at the farm?), Marcus slid on his boots and grabbed his wallet.

The Nissan stunk of marijuana and it burned his eyes. Carlos handed back a bottle of beer, and the car vibrated down the dirt road, soon reaching smooth asphalt streets. Never-ending walls flanked them while distorted trumpets blared from the speakers on either side of his head. Oscar tapped his hand on his knee to the music and faced out the window, and Carlos drummed his thumbs on the steering wheel. His eyes were wide open and bloodshot. Streetlights splashed yellow-orange over his face. Hugo turned around in the seat, and his whole face darkened with shadow. He asked Marcus how he liked México. Delgado sat with his long legs scrunched up in the seat behind Carlos, with a hood drooped over his eyes. Marcus drank two beers and had started in on the third when the car pulled into the parking lot of an apartment complex.

A row of three ten-story apartment buildings stood at the end of the lot. Carlos parked the car and swished the palms of his hands together.

"Vámonos," Carlos said. When he swept his smiling face across everyone in the back seat, his teeth gleamed. Carlos's appearance had changed. He had vibrant black hair slicked back, a subtle Roman nose, full purple lips, and Marcus couldn't look away. Carlos had beauty. Leroy, whom Marcus had considered a leader, had also had beauty. Marcus chugged the beer and stepped from the car.

He swayed across the parking lot. But Leroy, he thought, had the shoulders of a fullback. A layer of fat softened Carlos's chest and gut. Still, he thought, this is Oscar's brother, just as Leroy (*his head broken open, too moody and unsubtle to forgive me*) is mine. Nothing, he thought, not even having blood in common binds people together like shared witnessing of violence.

They all climbed a stairwell. Marcus gripped the guardrail with both hands and followed Oscar and the boys up several flights. Something pinched inside his hip. Oscar laid a hand on his shoulder and asked if he was all right because Marcus had been cringing. Marcus nodded.

The Nissan below shrunk more and more with every flight they climbed. The wind gusted across the lot and through the open stairwell. At the top floor, Marcus stopped, and his lungs burned. His hip throbbed. Carlos rapped his knuckles on a door, number 1001, and the door opened. A chain pulled taut across a woman's face. Carlos murmured.

Suddenly someone was manhandling Marcus towards the door. Carlos had slung his arm around him and ushered him forward. His warm breath stunk of beer and pot. Oscar made an "ooh" sound.

"El americano primero," Carlos said.

The girl who'd opened the door had yellow dyed hair, bangs falling over plucked eyebrows. She wore pink lipstick, a skintight t-shirt and shorts, which were scissor-snipped sweatpants. It was the girl from the bar; the scabs that had formed over the fingernail scratches had flaked away.

She turned and walked towards a door. Hugo, Delgado, and Oscar fell back while Carlos, still holding Marcus around the shoulder, whistled at the young woman's body and positioned Marcus before the doorframe. The girl opened the door and turned. Air that smelled of mold puffed out. She all at once lurched and clasped either side of Marcus's face. Her fingernails dug in as she meshed her lips into his, and without thinking Marcus thrust his hands against her chest. The young woman (had he really pushed her that hard?) flew back and landed on her backside. Her legs spread out in front of her. She leapt up, her face scarlet wrinkles, and punched. He bent forward, and she slashed nails across his face. She slapped his ear and tried to kick his genitals. She hammered his head, and the ringing in his ear deafened him.

Everyone retreated from the apartment. Carlos blurted the word, *pistola*, and they all scrambled down the stairs, soon abandoning Marcus, who hobbled out and down the stairwell and waited for the bullet to pierce his back and blow out a chunk of his chest.

When he had finally limped down to the parking lot, all the brothers stood with their backs pressed against the stairwell wall. Nobody wanted to step out in case the woman really did have a pistol. Oscar looked at Marcus, then shook his head and walked out into the parking lot. Blinking, Oscar turned towards the top floor, and his shoulders lifted as he dodged a hurled stiletto. Carlos, the brothers, Oscar, and Marcus hurried across the lot towards the Nissan. They were soon safe on the road, but Marcus's head was still ringing.

At the first stop sign, Carlos adjusted the rearview mirror to look into the back seat. "Damn, *Marc*us," he said. Everyone was quiet. Then Carlos chuckled, laughed harder. Oscar cupped a hand over his mouth.

"Pinche americano," Delgado said.

At that, laughter spluttered through Oscar's clasped hand. Hugo twisted around in the seat, a beer between his forefinger and thumb. Marcus took it, twisted off the cap, and drank. He huffed out a laugh, the car moving down unlighted, walled streets, and fingered his swollen eye.

The next afternoon, Marcus wandered down the Avenue of the Dead, a step ahead of Amora and Jesús, with the pyramid of the moon god behind, roped off for preservation efforts, and the pyramid of the sun god, earth lurching from earth, ahead. The sun glared through wisps of cloud, so everything had yellowed. As he neared, squinting from the sun, the pyramid inhaled, reptilian, until finally when Marcus stood at the foot of the worn stairs that led to the apex, it quivered, fragile.

"The pyramid and the moth," Marcus said. This combination of phrases struck him as though he'd uncovered a key. A key that helped him understand his feeling of having done this before, of having *known.* Or was it that the whole city around him, ruins of carved stone, reminded him of the time he and Leroy had climbed to the roof of the dormitory, the short-lived camp, back in Baghdad? There, too, the earth had rippled dusty and arid for miles, and the sun had burst through and spilled over the sky. They had peered off towards Baghdad, the outskirts of the Al-Salaam district, bombed out and smoking, a mile away, then they'd sprawled on their backs spread-eagle and let the concrete burn them through their t-shirts and desert camo pants. The sun had blistered his lips. The back of his eyelids had reddened as he listened to Leroy breathing beside him.

Now, Marcus's boot slipped into a depression in the first step. Last night, the moths had battered their faces against the light bulb in his room. A dozen of them had fluttered in by the time he'd returned from his final night out with Oscar and the boys. Clouds had stretched like cotton over the moon, so after Oscar replied, "Adiós, hermano," and slouched through the curtain, through the trail of trees, and was gone, Marcus had flicked off the light, and the ground had slanted, revolved, trembled in darkness. Back in Ohio, forgetting a brother had seemed an unforgivable lapse, but Oscar showed him forgetting was easy.

He climbed up the path. On either side of him, stones jutted from the angled wall, stones which once had anchored crimson stucco. This pyramid in its prime had shimmered, unreal, because the Aztec had chosen this place to serve, its pattern wasting nothing.

Marcus lifted the injured leg with both hands because it had numbed. At the top platform, he turned around. Amora mounted the pyramid with her dress swishing over her knees, and Jesús climbed a step behind.

Below crumbled the necropolis. The sun had numbed his lips, fell heavy on his shoulders, and licked his scalp like flame. The city underneath, the wrecked walls—it was all very similar. His father had made a farm. What had he made?

Jesús neared, then stepped away and fluttered near the edge of the precipice. Amora's sandaled feet shuffled until she stood beside him. She smelled of sweet soil.

BOOK 3

THE BIRTH

Again, our guardian is really both soldier and philosopher.
Plato, The Republic

CHAPTER 1

Black-purple streaked the sky, a sign of coming rain, and Marcus, having taken the bus from the airport to Antiguo's bus station, crouched outside beside a hobo. The hobo's bone-thin legs swam in desert fatigue pants.

Marcus rubbed his chin and wished he'd shaved. He leaned his head against the bricks and closed his eyes, and the sound of people walking past, of traffic, and of screeching bus brakes pulsed through droning wind. He opened his eyes at raindrops and wondered if he should wait for Leroy inside when, from around the corner, a man with sharp shoulders marched towards him. Leroy, his upper-body swollen from weightlifting, swaggered with a prosthetic leg.

Marcus stood up. "I was waiting for the van," he said.

Leroy wore a wife-beater, his skin had sun-darkened to black-gold, and his shoulders, chest, and arms bulged. A healthy layer of fat spread up into his cheeks and around his eyes. From his shorts, the prosthetic's titanium gleamed, polished, and sporty red foam softened the knee joint.

"I told you they was fitting a leg to me," Leroy said. "You find your brother?"

"I did," Marcus said.

"Can't believe you went alone," Leroy said and noticed the sleeping hobo.

"I knew what I was doing," Marcus said.

"Sure you did," Leroy said, and he stepped beside Marcus and nudged the man's boot.

"You know him?"

"We got the same shrink. Let's move, Berger." He glanced over the street. "Fore the beast come."

"Shrink?" Marcus said.

Leroy shrugged. "They say I was depressed."

"I thought you were just being an asshole." Marcus planted his fist into Leroy's shoulder.

The hobo peered through dusty eyelids. "Time already?" Berger said.

"Been time," Leroy said. "Come on."

"Time for what?" Marcus said.

"The street demo," Leroy said and opened his hands as though dropping something.

"A demo? Does your shrink approve of this?"

Leroy laughed, and Marcus knew that Leroy was back at last.

A gust swirled mist across Marcus's face as he lifted up Berger, whose breath smelled of vodka. Leroy lowered himself with his good leg and picked up the backpack. He flung the pack around his shoulder and looked almost like he had back in Baghdad when he'd been hitting the weights, sometimes for hours, often missing precious sleep.

On the heel of the prosthetic, Leroy pivoted and led them away from the bus station. Berger teetered on stiff legs, his arm hooked around Marcus's neck.

"Is this man really your friend?" Marcus said.

"He a vet," Leroy said over his shoulder, "but he still a puke."

Berger stirred at the insult and gave Leroy the middle finger.

By the time Marcus had dragged Leroy's acquaintance to the edge of a park, Berger had nearly fallen asleep, and rain had begun to fall. Most pedestrians trotted off along the sidewalk, pulling up collars or opening umbrellas, but Leroy, Marcus, and Berger mounted the rise to the park and crossed scorched grass. Parched trees and bushes rattled in the gusts of the growing storm. Leroy led the march, and the mechanized leg hummed as microprocessors balanced his weight. That leg, Marcus thought, was top of the line.

Leroy mumbled something the rain drowned out and pointed at a pavilion up ahead. Their feet splashed through standing water on the sidewalk, the rain seeping into Marcus's boots, and with Berger's weight straining his back, he wanted to lay the man down and catch his breath, but Leroy couldn't carry him.

At last they reached the pavilion, and once inside, Marcus laid Berger down on a picnic table, then plopped onto a bench. Wide puddles had already formed.

"I got to walk through the rain again," Leroy said. "You can stay here if you want and keep him from getting arrested." He bent forward to refasten the prosthetic.

"Then who's going to protect you?"

"Ain't illegal. We got a permit."

"Sounds radical."

Leroy swept his arm, and sighing, Marcus shouldered the backpack and left Berger passed out behind.

For several minutes, they traipsed through pines that trembled in the storm, needles crunching underfoot, and when they'd passed the trees, brick buildings appeared through the rain. He and Leroy slid down the rise, crossed a street, and walked along the sidewalk. No cars swished down the water-swollen road, but ahead, traffic churned on a four-laned main street in either direction. He and Leroy splashed through the water, the area a run-down industrial district, and turned a corner towards chanting.

In a row, people hooded in plastic ponchos thrust signs at passing traffic. *"Money for schools and education, not for war..."* The line of protesters wound along the curb for half a block. Leroy clasped the slumped shoulder of an elderly lady, whose gray curls clung to her face, and greeted her, and then a man who'd been holding signs on the ground between his knees glanced at Leroy's soaked body and scrambled to pull extra ponchos from a duffle bag. He handed one to each of them.

"This is Marcus," Leroy said, "a comrade of mine from Ohio."

Marcus shook the man's milky hand. "I'm Toby," the man said and handed Marcus a poncho. "Great to have you."

Leroy slipped on the plastic coat and took a sign from Toby, then swaggered to the end of the line and joined the chant. Traffic splashed by, and horns honked. Marcus pulled on his poncho and also took a sign. He caught up with Leroy, keeping the board down at his side, and shivered a step behind the others.

Beside Leroy, a young man jiggled a poster over his head. He gripped it with both hands and waved it at a passing car. The driver of the car made a gesture, a fist with his thumb jabbing downward, and the young man chanted: *"... NOT for war..."* His glasses fogged up from his breath.

For fifteen minutes, Marcus stood beside Leroy, never lifting his own sign, which, when he finally looked, read

War is Big Bu$ine$$. Some people in passing traffic honked horns in support, but many shouted obscenities out cracked windows. A salty mist lingered over the road from swishing tires, and the rain slammed down. Leroy steadied the sign in front of his chest and recited the chant.

"Who are these people?" Marcus asked.

"Folk from the peace center."

The young man with foggy glasses lifted his sign at a pickup truck. The driver showed the middle finger, which seemed to make the young man chant louder. Marcus couldn't see what Leroy had in common with these people, and he feared Leroy didn't know he was probably being paraded around as this group's token vet.

After another half hour, the group's chanting ended, and they milled around shaking hands before departing. Toby came by and spoke with Leroy in the rain.

"Keep the ponchos," he said. "Nice meeting you, Marcus." He waved his hand.

During their walk back through the park, amid the pines, Marcus asked Leroy how he'd happened to join the organization.

"It's good folk," Leroy said.

"You sure about that? You were the only black dude there."

"Ah," Leroy said and waved his hand. "Don't mean nothing."

"Look, I just hate the idea of people using you."

Leroy winced, limping. "It ain't that way."

"I mean, they don't know you," Marcus said. "How do you know you're not their poster boy?"

Leroy stopped and lifted his hands. "I know what I'm doing, man."

Grimacing, Leroy turned and hobbled towards an overflowing fountain and looked as though he would dip his hands into the water and wash his face, but he halted. Coming up behind him, Marcus realized why. Rain water welled from the basin, and the fountain teemed with pale-skinned frogs.

The next day, Marcus slouched in the third row of the bus's right column. Nobody sat beside him, so he leaned over and shut his eyes. He sipped coffee when the bus stopped in Roswell, and he slurped water from a fountain in Clovis. He didn't eat. His wallet, empty, stayed in his back pocket, with only his driver's license inside.

On the third day of travel, the bus stopped in St. Louis. Marcus sat on a bench, one of several that faced glass doors to the bus bay, and rested his head in his hands. What would Leroy's parents think? *They probably agree with Leroy. Leroy's grievance, after all, has strengthened him.* Still, he wanted Leroy away from that group.

A man with his fists shoved into his pockets walked up to Marcus and asked if anyone was sitting there. He wore blue jeans and a denim jacket, and after Marcus said the spot was empty, the man held out his hand to shake, gazing blurry-eyed through bangs. With his narrow face, flared nostrils, and beard, the man resembled a goat. He introduced himself as Mike.

"Marcus."

The man sat down. "Going to Indianapolis, Marcus?" He had the voice of a man who'd smoked daily for decades.

"Cleveland."

"Richmond myself," Mike said. "To meet my wife," he added as if talking to himself.

Mike reached into his jacket pocket and pulled out a flask. He asked Marcus if he wanted a drink and peered, waiting for an answer. Marcus knew he'd better accept, so he gulped down a little, and the gin bubbled in his empty stomach.

When it was time to board, Marcus walked bent forward, holding himself around the abdomen, and the man followed closely and sat beside him.

"Seven and a half hours," Mike said, settling into the seat, "until Richmond and the bed of the woman I love."

The bus moved along city streets until reaching the freeway. Mike guzzled from the flask and tried to give Marcus more until he noticed Marcus was in pain. "Hey, you all right?"

"Haven't eaten much lately," Marcus said.

At this, the man pulled a pouch of beef jerky from his jacket and handed it over. The bag was warm from being against the man's body, and after Marcus folded the pouch open, he pinched some and threw it into his mouth. While he chewed, salt spread and tingled, and his tongue searched out every last fiber of beef along his gums.

"Now take more of this," the man said. "Got plenty." While Marcus pretended to swig from the flask, the man stared. "Get into some kind of accident?"

Marcus handed the flask back. He paused, wondering if he should make up a lie, but the man had given him jerky and gin, was on his way to visit his wife, and they'd never meet again, so he told the stranger the truth: a bereaved father's suicide disfigured him and his buddy.

"Why'd the dude do it?" the man asked.

"We killed some people the day before," Marcus said. "Civilians."

"That's bogus, man." Mike took a long drink. "My old man seen me put into military school. Those animals used to have fun with us, know what I mean? But they never got me. Fought too hard." Mike swung his arms to simulate a fistfight. It looked like a breaststroke in slow motion.

And the man mumbled on, saying he'd ditched out on parole to see his wife, who lived in Richmond with their eight-year-old son. He loved that woman, and he was going to make it like it was before they'd locked him up. Next he described working in a meatpacking plant for minimum wage. Prison, he said, made him think people ought to stick with their own. "But you're all right," he added, before telling how his beloved father, when Mike was ten, taught him to slit the throats of dogs and pour gasoline in a car's interior if you want to torch it to the frame. After talking, he wore himself out and dozed. Marcus also closed his eyes.

When he awoke, it was four thirty in the morning, and the bus had stopped to pick up passengers in Dayton. They'd already passed through Richmond, and Mike, along with Marcus's wallet, was gone.

CHAPTER 2

Marcus's mother picked him up from the Ashtabula bus station in the morning. It was the last week of May, and lakeside humidity made his breathing shallow.

His mother stopped the Cavalier outside the bus station doors. During his absence, she'd changed her hairstyle. She wore it even shorter, jet-black (stray strands of gray now gone) and fingered back in chic tufts. Marcus's image reflected in the passenger side window. His hair bristled from his head in a crown. He slipped the backpack off his shoulder and opened the door.

His mother hugged him and brushed her hand over his cheek. She put the car into drive and sniffled. "You need a haircut," she said.

Marcus dropped the backpack into the back seat. "I see you got one."

"It's old," she said, "had it when you was born." She opened her fingers off the steering wheel then gripped down again. "I brought you muffins." In the console, tinfoil housed warm blueberry muffins and he stuffed one into his mouth. Three more remained, so he scarfed them down as well. As they drove through Ashtabula, his mother squinted as though reminiscing.

Without warning, she pulled the car into a plaza and stopped before a barbershop.

"Now?" he said. He licked crumbs off his lip.

"Kia Winslow's graduation party's today," his mother said and gave him a twenty-dollar bill. "Last Sunday, when she asked about you, the poor girl looked sick." His mother's eyes flashed away. "Didn't you ever call?"

A teenager in the parking lot, beyond Marcus's mother, shoved a shopping cart into a port and spat on the ground. "I never called," Marcus said, "but I should've." He stared out the windshield. He whiffed bitter earth around the outbuilding and farmhouse. Flower fields tumbled.

Marcus stepped from the barbershop and entered a pharmacy, where he bought a half-gallon of bottled water. When he stepped back outside his mother's Cavalier was idling at the curb. He opened the door, slid in, and found his mother had bought yellow roses and a card. "From both of us," she said. She took him to the lakeside cottage, insisting he clean himself up.

Two hours later, Marcus and his mother parked almost a block away from Kia's house, cars crowding both sides of the street.

Marcus carried the card while his mother grasped the bundle of flowers, and they walked along the sweet-smelling pine trees and into Kia's backyard. Gray-white smoke lifted off a sizzling barbeque grill, and children in the middle of the yard swatted a shuttlecock with badminton rackets. Just outside the back porch, a tent sheltered picnic tables of food, under which several people lingered, holding paper plates under their chins with one hand, sandwiches in the other. Among them, Kia held a Styrofoam cup with both hands and sipped from it while listening to a man, perhaps one of her uncles, who had a beer. Marcus followed his mother towards Kia. By the grill across the yard, Nancy Winslow squeezed the bicep of an athletic man wearing sunglasses and dashed towards the tent. She tried to cut Marcus and his mother off.

"Nancy Winslow," Marcus's mother said. "Congrats, girl!" She pushed the flowers into Marcus's chest. "Take these to the graduate," she said and imprisoned Nancy in a hug.

Kia reddened when Marcus neared. Her uncle noticed and also regarded Marcus.

"I have gifts," Marcus said. Kia was drinking red fruit juice.

Behind Marcus, Nancy called to Kia. "Come say hello to Missus Green."

Marcus's mother raised her hand and shouted a hello. Kia waved and glanced at Marcus. She wore a tank top that showed off her athletic shoulders and slender neck.

"Ain't you going to introduce me?" the man with the beer said.

"This is Marcus," she said. "Marcus, Uncle Frank."

"Franklin," the man said and shook hands.

"Gifts go inside," Kia said. "Come on." She told her uncle she'd be back and turned towards the sliding glass door. She and Marcus went inside.

In the relative silence of the living room, they stood before the couch laden with cards and presents. Kia set her cup down on top of the television. Her shirt clung to her stomach, and she and Marcus faced each other in the middle of the room.

"You worried me," she said and snatched the flowers. She squeezed them in fists, then relaxed. "Couldn't you have called?"

A giggling boy pawed at the sliding glass door and tugged it open. Two other laughing children, a boy and girl, chased the first child into the living room, and their running shook the house. The children scrambled down the hall towards the front door. When Marcus turned back to Kia, she crashed into his chest and pinned his arms to his body.

Fettering him, with the flowers prickling his back, she spoke in a husky whisper.

"I need you to call me from now on," she said, "because I'm pregnant."

She lifted her face from his chest, and Marcus held his breath, meeting Kia's strained gaze.

"You can understand that, can't you?" she said.

Marcus cupped her hips and drew their bodies together. He believed he could feel, just above Kia's navel, a solid lump both their stomachs cushioned. "Of course I can," he said, kissing her flushed forehead. "Who wouldn't?"

He slept on his mother's couch that night.

Until morning, waves crested on shore, endless concussions.

Restless, he dreamed he was crouching in the sand outside, a violet void (a storm that groaned) offshore. He scrambled up the hill and hammered his fist against the door. The house was Amora's house, and nobody let him in.

Five o'clock the next morning, he lifted himself from the couch and showered. The day before, Kia had told him her mother's car was in the shop, so he'd volunteered to take her to work. He wanted to let Nancy know that, at the graduation party, Kia had told him she was pregnant.

Nancy wore a t-shirt and jeans and held a mug of coffee while she strode down the walkway towards the Subaru.

"Austinburg El.," she said, so Marcus put the car in gear and started.

In Austinburg, he dropped her off at the school, and before she stepped from the car, he blurted, "I'm going to look for work this morning."

Nancy's jaw sagged but her mouth, expressionless, was shut.

"Kia told me," he said.

Nancy spoke in a voice adults use when humoring adolescent dreamers—a gentle, singsong voice. "Okay, Marcus."

She shut the door and passed a thin man smoking a cigarette outside. The man pressed the insole of each boot together as if it were winter and reminded Marcus of someone he'd recently met—the man, Mike, on the bus. The man greeted Nancy then watched her from behind.

Marcus put the car in gear and went to hunt for work.

He had to find something, anything. Nancy doubted him. Who wouldn't? He hadn't had enough time to prove his commitment, so he would take the first job, no matter what it was.

On his way towards Ashtabula, he turned into a truck stop that had gasoline and diesel pumps. He pumped gas and read a sign by the doors, *Maintence Man Wanted*, and laughed at the misspelling.

After getting gas, he went inside to apply.

Marcus's would-be boss, Gayle, took him to a narrow backroom office a half hour later. She explained the store's old maintenance man had struck out for Las Vegas. Gayle had the face of a bird, droopy eyelids, an angular nose, and lips she'd chewed away to lipstick-painted slivers. She spoke in monotone, passionless. It was something she must've developed through years of overseeing short-timers. Marcus nodded at everything she said. He would be different. He would work dutifully no matter how long he stayed.

On his way back to the Subaru, he read over the checklist Gayle demanded he follow without deviation:

> change garbage bags (inside and outside store);
> measure level of fuel in tanks;
> clean restrooms (men's and women's, wear plastic gloves, sweep and mop, supply);
> stock coolers;
> stock shelves;
> sweep and mop store floors;
> sweep up trash from parking lot (esp. cigarette butts) and pick up trash in the peripheral grass and ditches (wear gloves when cleaning behind where semis parked: beware of bodily fluids, syringes);
> wash down pumps;
> re-clean restrooms (see number 3);
> report to supervisor.

That evening, from his mother's house, he phoned his father. He wanted to visit him, that he knew, but he had no idea what he'd say. Everything needed to be all right with his old man. Kia was pregnant, and Marcus was going to need help.

As it turned out, Marcus had called at a good time.

"The oak out front's leaning towards the house," his father said. They needed to down it, or it would wreck the roof by fall.

That Saturday, Marcus pulled into his father's drive at ten in the morning. Sunlight struggled through overcast clouds.

In the front yard, the black oak resembled a gnarled, cupped hand. Marcus parked the Subaru, stuffed his work gloves into his back pocket, and approached the tree. Mold had encrusted the trunk bark and killed most branches. Only one branch had survived, and it sprouted yellow-green leaves, bristles sharpening leaf tips. Weakened, the tree shivered in every breeze.

His father shuddered open the garage door, greeted Marcus in a grunt, and bore a ladder and chainsaw towards the spot. He wore goggles and leather gloves, and Marcus hurried forward to relieve him of the ladder. After Marcus lugged it across the yard, he opened it near the trunk's base, underneath the lowest branch, and his father handed him a pair of goggles. Marcus slipped them on and stuffed his hands into the gloves.

"Let's down the unruly thing," his father said, "before the rain starts." He climbed the ladder while Marcus steadied it. At the top, he yanked the chainsaw's cord. The saw snorted and died, so he adjusted the choke and pulled again. The saw whined and vibrated the air.

It sank into the branch and flung chips and dust while Marcus gripped the ladder. The motor shook the steel and numbed his hands. Soon his father shouted a warning, and the first branch fell. The saw idled as his father climbed down.

At the bottom, he handed Marcus the tool. It trembled in Marcus's hands. His father wiped sweat from his upper lip with the back of his glove.

"So," his father said, the safety goggles blurring his eyes, "how'd he look?"

The sudden frankness made it hard for Marcus to speak. "Like hell," he finally said.

"There's many ways to live," his father replied and turned back to work. He dragged the ladder across muddy earth and positioned it beneath another branch.

This time Marcus climbed up. At the top, he braced himself and leaned with outstretched arms. Pulling the trigger, he nudged the spinning blade's teeth into the branch and lacerated its bark. The saw shot splinters, and dust collected in his nostrils as the spinning teeth gnawed through the wood and amputated the branch. The branch cut, Marcus loosened his hold on the trigger, and his father told him to kill the motor, so he did before climbing down.

Together they dragged the felled branches away from the trunk.

When they met at the trunk's base again, Marcus cleared his throat to speak. They stood facing each other amid a mist of sawdust and the sweet smell of severed wood.

"I'm going to be a father," Marcus said.

His father shaped his mouth as if he'd been struck. "Who?"

"Kia Winslow."

His father pinched a glove's finger and pulled out his hand.

"I *want* to," Marcus said. "I found a job, good enough for now, and enrolled for classes at the Ashtabula campus."

"Marcus," his father said, "this is major." Leaning forward, he chopped the bare hand into the palm of the gloved one. "You'll need to stay vigilant about yourself and what you do."

"I will," Marcus said.

"You'll need to stay organized from now on." He shaped his hand into a blade and hacked. "From now on, you'll need to stay consistent."

"I will," Marcus said. "I *will*."

That first month, every weekday morning Marcus woke at four thirty, brewed coffee, showered, and fried eggs before driving to the truck stop. He arrived at a quarter till six and, after a day of maintaining the grounds as Gayle prescribed, at two o'clock flew to Kia's house. He then showered and strode with a towel around his waist into Kia's room, where she sometimes tore the towel off, and they lay together, murmuring or quietly embracing, until Nancy returned home from work after four.

By the beginning of July, he'd saved enough money to buy Kia a promise ring (he deposited most of every check into a savings account). He gave it to her after the pre-natal visit, when they'd heard the baby's heartbeat by Doppler.

By middle August, he'd made a down payment on a diamond engagement ring.

Mornings were cooler now. For the first time that year, frost crystallized on the Subaru windshield. It happened the last week of August, on the morning of the day they'd scheduled a mid-pregnancy ultrasound.

The twelve-foot measuring stick wobbled in his hand as he walked across the truck lot, the sky black and starry overhead, towards the underground fuel tanks. He dropped the stick and pried off every lid in the row. He then walked back to the first hole, pulled the latex work gloves tighter around his fingers, and plunged his hand in. The plastic cap to the fuel tank gave and twisted off, and the smell of gasoline wafted up. Marcus held the stick with both hands and dipped it into the tank until it touched bottom. He held it for a moment, and when he lifted the stick, the level of gasoline read forty inches. He wiped off the gasoline with blue paper towels, which came from the dispensers where squeegees bobbed in windshield washing fluid.

The afternoon before, he'd snuggled against Kia's naked backside and felt her vibrating voice.

"Do you want a son," Kia had said, "or a daughter?"

At that, Marcus realized he'd been seeing the child, all along, as a boy. "I can't say for sure," he said. "What about you?"

"A girl," Kia said.

"Me too."

Kia had rolled over. "Liar."

Under the morning sky, with highway traffic swishing along Interstate 90 behind him, Marcus lifted the stick from the tank and wiped it with a towel before he shuffled over to the next tank, twisted off the cap, and sank the stick in again. It hit bottom, but unlike the first and second tank, the third tank was full because nobody bought premium anymore.

At the next hole, he measured diesel levels. He dropped the stick and had to wipe it and drop it again. The stick sank forever into the massive cistern. He pinched the final inch of the stick with his fingertips, his knuckles against the tank mouth.

("I want what you want," Marcus had said. "Anyway girls are smarter, and sweeter." He pulled her closer, but she drew coquettishly back.)

The final measurement read eighty-three. He slipped the gloves off and dropped them on the ground before pulling a piece of cardboard from his vest pocket, which bore his name in thread. He scribbled down the numbers for Gayle.

The hospital waiting room always chilled Marcus. Kia flipped through a magazine while he stared ahead at a painting, which showed a sailboat dipping behind the horizon. The sky and water were white, and black-gray rocks, like cuts of ice, formed the shore.

"Guess what," Kia had said in the car. She beamed.

"What?" They were crossing the Ashtabula River.

"*Guess.*"

"You ate better today?"

"No," she said, "I *felt* her."

Marcus cupped Kia's belly. "Her?"

Soon a nurse called Marcus and Kia back into a room. Marcus followed Kia and, once inside, helped her slip on the gown. She stepped up into a reclining chair and uncovered her abdomen. The nurse rubbed gel on Kia's belly before applying the transducer.

"Observe the screen," the nurse said.

On the monitor, an ashen image materialized of their baby reposing in the womb, frosty-blue as though frozen over. With her free arm, the nurse pointed and counted ten fingers and ten toes.

"Boy or girl?" Marcus said, half to himself.

"Too early to tell for sure," the nurse answered, "but so far it looks like you two have a healthy girl."

Marcus knelt beside Kia and gazed at the monitor. Their cheeks touched, and leaning forward, Marcus felt the bulge of the engagement ring in his pocket. The thought inspired him, so he pulled out the ring and knelt.

The nurse looked at Marcus. Then Kia looked, confused, and Marcus opened the ring case.

"Can I—Kia, will you marry me?"

The nurse threw her hands over her mouth, and Kia nodded holding out her hand so that Marcus could slip on the ring. He stood and kissed her temple and smelled her hair. She rubbed his hand with her thumb so hard it hurt the veins. Then they turned again towards the monitor that showed the coming baby.

All at once, the monitor went blank. Marcus stared ahead, confused by what he saw until he recognized the images in the monitor were his and Kia's reflection.

Marcus took Kia to his grandmother's house to share the news and to do minor yard work. Through the cloudless sky, the sun burned through his t-shirt while, inside the house, his grandmother was probably serving Kia ice cream and half-thawed strawberries.

After cleaning up the flowerbed, he passed once around her house to pick up fallen sticks and a plastic bag blown under a hedge before going to the back door. He went inside and found Kia sitting at the kitchen table with the sun yellow-orange on her shoulder, his grandmother beside her. As he'd done his entire youth, after entering his grandmother's house, he sat down at the kitchen table to await the dessert she insisted on serving him.

"Heard you moved in with your mother," his grandmother said, standing from the table. (Marcus knew better than to ask if he ought to serve himself.) His grandmother wore a dark-blue gown that hid the contours of her body, as her skin hid growths of cancer.

"It's closer to Kia," he said.

"Mm," she said and opened the freezer to remove a plastic tub from the back. Holding the dessert with both hands, she shuffled to the counter. From the cupboard, she took a ceramic soup bowl, and from a drawer below, she took a spoon. She ran the spoon under hot water before cutting slivers from the surface. With an index finger she dropped the strips off the spoon into the bowl, then jabbed the spoon into the ice cream, slid the bowl onto the table towards him, and put the tub away.

As soon as his grandmother had eased herself down, wincing, into the kitchen chair, the phone rang.

"I got it, Grandma," Marcus said and jumped up. The phone was in the living room, where the air felt cool because of the thirty live plants his grandmother had crowded before the picture window. He sat down in his grandmother's creaking wicker chair and grabbed the receiver. It was his mother.

"Marcus," his mother said, "you in any kind of trouble?"

When he heard his mother say that, on impulse his eyes flashed in the direction of Kia.

"Marcus," his mother said, "a police officer was just here, asking where you been."

"Why?"

"He wanted to know when I last saw you, and I told him you been living here, and he asked how long and I told him that."

Outside the front window, a police cruiser eased to a stop immediately in front of his grandmother's house.

"I'll call you back, Mama."

An officer wearing sunglasses stepped from the car and walked over to the Subaru. He checked the license plate and looked towards the house.

Kia and his grandmother were silent in the kitchen, but the living room wall hid him from them.

"Who was it, dear?" his grandmother called.

"Mama," he said and knew his voice had given him away, but there was no time. He crept forward and took hold of the front door's jiggly antique knob. The door opened with a click.

"Everything all right?" his grandmother called. "Ice cream melting."

Marcus, with all his body outside on the porch, poked his head back through the doorway.

"Be right in." He quietly closed the door and hurried down the porch.

From the other side of the police cruiser, the officer (long legs in ironed slacks) strode around the back of the car.

"Lose your license a while back, Mister Green?" The officer held a notepad and a pen.

"It was stolen, with my wallet."

"Know the man who took it?"

"He told me his name. It was Mike, but I'd never met him before."

The officer's brown biceps bulged in the short sleeves as he scribbled in the notepad. "When's the last time you made contact with this man?"

"I never made contact. He stole my wallet."

"Were you in Lexington last week?"

"Lexington? You mean Kentucky?"

"Mister Green, we think a wanted felon used your driver's license to check into a motel in Lexington."

"Mine was stolen. I got a new one. You can check."

The cop smiled. "I did."

Marcus glanced back at the house. He spoke more softly. "What's he wanted for?"

"Murder, of his wife."

"What should I do?"

"Is there any reason this man would try to contact you?"

Marcus squinted. *Contact me?* "I don't know."

"If you happen to see this man, give us a call immediately, all right Mister Green?"

The officer left his card with Marcus, and his heels clicked over the asphalt as he returned to the cruiser.

CHAPTER 4

For three more months, Marcus followed Gayle's list, and slowly he stopped scrutinizing everyone coming through the truck stop who vaguely resembled the man who'd sat beside him on the bus.

Just after Mike had done it, the story had been all over the news. As the story went, Mike had skipped out on parole and gone to Richmond, but he'd found his wife had fled. His wife had found out Mike was coming and didn't want to live with that temper again, so she sent her eight-year-old boy with her sister to Indianapolis. It took her a few days, but she moved the bulk of her belongings into storage and herself fled from Richmond. It had taken Mike three months to track her down in Indianapolis, and when he finally had, he'd murdered the woman he'd told Marcus, over and over, he had loved.

With time, Marcus reasoned that no matter how deranged or desperate Mike was, he'd never come to Ohio. Still, some nights he squirmed awake, damning himself for opening up to Mike on the bus.

On a Thursday in September, Marcus clocked out and spotted, across the parking lot, the man who'd stolen his identity. Mike leaned against a blue, banged up Ford Escort, smoking a cigarette and pumping gas, and Marcus unlocked and dove into the Subaru. He ducked down and eased the car door closed, and he watched.

When the dull-blue Escort moved from the gas pump bay, Marcus straightened in the seat. The Escort's engine revved up, and the car scraped bottom on the asphalt edge as it turned and headed towards Orwell. The car rolled across the overpass that spanned interstate traffic, and Marcus prayed the Escort's turn signal would blink and the car would turn down the ramp to Interstate 90. Instead, the narrow car wobbled along the state route that, within fifteen miles, would lead to the farmhouse. Marcus gripped the steering wheel, started the engine, and followed.

Once on the road, Marcus shouted. His face and chest burned. It had to be a nightmare, he bleated. He pounded fists against the ceiling.

Far ahead, the Escort rolled southward. The car's crooked alignment wrenched the front wheels leftward. Marcus neared, could read the license plate number. The car had Kentucky plates, and wind cut through the killer's hair. But, Marcus realized, his father would be at work. He could lag back, so he lifted his foot off the gas and let the Escort drift ahead.

The misaligned Escort wobbled in its lane, and its driver looked drunk or sleepy. Several times dust exploded off the right berm, and the car swerved back into the lane. The sun blazed overhead.

The Escort's brake lights flashed in front of the farmhouse. Marcus sped up as the Escort pulled in and yanked the wheel to the left. Marcus had pulled into the drive of the widow, Myrtle Williams.

Her driveway slanted upward and leveled out in front of a garage. He parked the Subaru in the shade and ducked down, tilting the mirror to watch Mike. Pine trees lined the farmhouse property and limited his view to half the Escort.

The killer walked up the steps to the farmhouse porch and creaked open the screen door. He lifted his arm, knocked, and scanned his surroundings. Mike waited before stepping to the edge of the porch. He shoved fists into his pockets and gazed, it seemed, across the yard and at the Subaru. Myrtle Williams, white hair pulled back, nudged open the screen door to her kitchen. Sun whitened her face and yellowed loose skin beneath her eyes. "Who's there?"

Marcus opened the car door. "It's Marcus, ma'am."

"Marcus?" Myrtle hunched forward, listening.

"Ed Green's grandson," Marcus said. He stepped from the car. At the farmhouse across the street, the Escort was backing into the turnaround and moving through potholes towards the road.

"Ed died," Myrtle said.

"Sorry to bother you, Missus Williams." As he spoke, the Escort gained speed and headed back down the state route. The driver turned to look, a moment of recognition, but kept going. "I thought," Marcus said, "I'd locked myself out, but it turns out I have the house key after all." Marcus walked back to the car and started the engine. He reversed onto the road and turned into the farmhouse drive.

Once stopped, he got out and trotted across the driveway. In the front yard, sawdust sprinkled the grass around the jagged stump where the sick oak had been.

Myrtle Williams, still standing in her doorway, watched with her hands fumbling at the screen door handle.

"It's all right," Marcus called, waving his arm over his head, impatient to run into the farmhouse and call the cops.

Myrtle drew back into her house like the head of a turtle.

CHAPTER 5

One evening, in his English literature class at the Ashtabula campus of Kent State, Marcus argued with his classmates and the professor.

"The speaker," Marcus said, "says he *came* up to the water's surface, but he should've said he *went*. We go towards something whereas something comes to us, so since there's no one else in the scene, the verb kind of splits the speaker in two. It's like he's going to a part of himself that's waiting at the surface."

Hemingway's narrator had injured a guy in a bar fight and, escaping, heard from a person on the street that a man down the road had just been murdered. Marcus was arguing that murder-guilt haunted Hemingway's first-person narrator. He wondered how anyone could read about the narrator trying to loot a ship without making this connection, without considering the possibility of the narrator's guilt. "Looting a ship's a metaphor," Marcus continued. "He's really praying. Praying to harmonize conscience and self." While Marcus spoke, everyone around him squinted at the page and shook their heads. One guy lifted fingers to his mouth and smoked an invisible doobie.

"But that," Marcus's professor said, pointing at the book of short stories as if the proof were written on its binding, "isn't what the story *says*." Several students grunted in agreement and lifted their faces from their books. They leaned back, straightened in their seats, and listened. "What the story *says* is that he knows all along that he's merely cut the guy, albeit cut him severely, across the arm."

"You're wrong," Marcus shot back. "Hemingway may not have spelled it out, but he sure as hell writes it."

A week later, October was on its way out as Marcus's fingers rattled over a keyboard in the university library. He typed his words angrily, venting his frustration into an essay on Hemingway that he doubted his professor would fully accept.

After some final edits he printed the paper. While he waited, he checked his email and found his marine buddy Phil Michaels had written.

Hey Marcus I got computer time and there was no one else to write to. I should'nt a wrote you since you never wrote me back. Well, we're doing the same shit different day. I'm single now again, Cindy divorced me. In her head she blamed me for the problems with us trying to have kids. So it goes. Leroy told me your getting married. Things are crazy here since the dandelion heads got popped off. I just wanna know what old Nick thought he was doing. Well I better go I'm on patrol tonight. Yea, fun times. By the way we got a real punching bag finally. You lucky fuck I wish I was jerking off at home. They put something in the food so we can't wank I'm convinced of it. They probably figured how much a year it saves. Philbarmonic

Marcus burst out laughing and some students around him gawked. He continued to snicker to himself as he walked to the community printer and retrieved his essay. After returning to the computer, he responded to Phil.

I'm getting married next week. Leroy's the best man and is flying northeast this Saturday. We're going to cut up before I'm married for good. Get leave and visit. Marcus

He almost clicked the send button, but he paused. He reread Phil's message. He read the part about Phil's divorce.

What was it Leroy had said? *Three kids in a row, all born dead.*

"Kia's pregnant," Marcus wrote, and he stared at the words. The library windows shuddered. Behind him, outside the ground floor window, Lake Erie churned mile-wide waves towards shore. Leafless trees quivered while wind howled.

He sent the email, and afterwards he drove along the blowing lake, steadying the Subaru's steering wheel against the wind.

Later that day, he and Kia visited the Ashtabula hospital for a routine checkup. Kia had been dutifully monitoring the baby's movements and recording how many times and when the baby kicked each day. Once they were inside, a petite Filipino doctor pressed a stethoscope to Kia's swollen belly and handed the earpieces to Kia. At the sound of movement inside her, Kia's eyes widened and she blushed, turning to Marcus.

"You want to listen?"

He'd been staring at her stomach and shook his head as if awakening. "Of course," he said, and he placed the stethoscope to Kia's belly and listened. He could hear movement, which meant the child was alive, but as he focused on the little racing heartbeat he became convinced the child was terrified.

Kia was dressing when Marcus slipped out the door and caught up to the doctor, gripping her arm.

"Is the baby all right?" Marcus said.

The doctor ripped her arm from him. "Don't touch me," she said, walking away without another word.

During the car ride home, Kia asked him what was wrong. "You're worrying me," she said.

He almost told Kia then about Phil's wife. About others he'd known in the Corps who had returned from service only to sire children that hadn't lived past the womb. But what good would come from telling her without first finding out more? The way it was, she ate well and, as far as he knew, thought of herself in relation to the child in the right way. Sunny specialists in brochures and birthing sessions encouraged Kia's thinking this way, the *right* way. She nourished the child, and her body kept its place sanitary.

Marcus parked the Subaru in front of Kia's house.

"You're really scaring me," she said. She didn't want to get out.

Marcus mumbled something about Leroy's getting into town.

"Can't you—? We're getting married, Marcus." She held her hand palm up, entreating. "In five days," she said. "Why can't you talk to me, even a little?"

Marcus slouched back in the driver's seat, rain sprinkling over the car's roof and windshield, and held Kia's hand.

He told her about the swaying man and his wailing with the child in his arms, about the bomb on the man's chest and how either his or the child's finger bone had burrowed itself into Marcus's hip.

He told her about the woman whose robe, bloodied, had looked violet.

What he didn't tell was what bothered him most, his worry over their child's fate and the reckless wandering of Mike, who had Marcus's license.

In the end, Kia stepped from the car, unsatisfied. Cradling her abdomen, she watched him drive away.

He arrived at Cleveland Hopkins Airport an hour later.

Marcus waited for Leroy by the baggage claim belt. He'd had trouble seeing during the drive to Cleveland because the rain had swirled into the windshield the entire time. Behind him, rain still splattered over the walkway.

He needed to know what Leroy knew about Phil's ex-wife and the three stillbirths. He needed to find out Leroy's opinion on Kia.

Finally, Leroy's bulky frame emerged in a crowd of people. Leroy lifted his arm towards Marcus, and his voice boomed out:

"You need to *eat* something."

With Leroy beside him, Marcus drove eastward on Interstate 90. He cruised along Lake Road once they reached Ashtabula. Clouds blotted the sky. Marcus moved along the lake, and wind gusted against the driver's side door, shoving him towards the ditch. Sunlight sometimes streaked through fissures, and when that happened, light clarified everything around them, the road, the leafless trees, the foaming lake, and sunrays reflected off Leroy's ankle. The titanium limb showed from the bottom of Leroy's pants.

Leroy told Marcus he'd left the organization and joined a new one.

"We went to Los Angeles," Leroy said, "and homeless vets was all around us." They'd traveled in a van a second time to Los Angeles and rallied together the homeless veterans. "Just fed them," Leroy said. "And ones we could salvage came back to Antiguo with us and also to Dallas last month." Leroy trailed off after Marcus stayed silent. Marcus was thinking about Phil Michaels. They drove along a stretch of the lake where purple-black clouds hung low.

"I heard from Phil," Marcus said at last. He passed the Ashtabula campus of Kent State and continued east. He was going to a bar and grill in the harbor area named The Anchor, where an actual quarter-ton anchor leaned against the wall behind the bar. "You heard from anyone?" He wanted to know about Squirrel Reed's child that, as they spoke, was growing inside Nurse Sheila.

"A few people," Leroy said.

Barren black trees sprawled around blocks of city houses. Marcus parked in front of the bar, and as soon as he stepped outside, salty wind made him shiver. Leroy pulled himself from the low-riding car and thrust the door closed. He gazed blurry-eyed at the middle-space in front of him and swaggered around the Subaru front end as though towards a brawl. Marcus led him across the street.

Bells jingled in the doorway when Marcus stepped in. A man in a flannel shirt leaned over a beer at the bar and stared. The bartender, a bleach-blond wraith of a woman, also watched them enter. Marcus walked along the bar and slid into a bench in the corner booth, and the bartender floated towards them. Leroy turned his back to the seat, and with one arm on the table and the other on the booth's frame, he lowered himself, then gripped the titanium leg with both hands to pull it under. The bartender asked what they wanted, and they ordered sandwiches, Marcus the BLT, Leroy the steakburger.

"So," Leroy said, "what's new with Phil?"

"Stillbirths," Marcus said.

Leroy turned towards the window beside their booth and snorted. "Same old Marcus." He hunched his shoulders forward and smirked. "Listen," Leroy said, and opened his hands as though letting something fly from him, "it ain't a secret. You know that. You just need to hear it, don't you? We poisoned. Something we stuck our noses into makes it harder to have kids. What you going to do? Infect her with your own damn doubts? Tell your wife and do like you did—?"

To me, Leroy was going to say.

Leroy dropped his arms to his sides and leaned back, facing out the window. "Fact is," Leroy said, "no one know what it is. Might've got into us in basic, one of the shots, or it might be like some others say, that it's the dust we was hacking on."

The bartender brought them their sandwiches. She stared at the table and placed the plates in front of them.

"Anything else?"

"Yeah," Leroy said, "a pitcher of Bud."

The woman checked their driver's licenses and glided behind the bar.

"Damn," Leroy said, slouching back in the booth and putting his identification card away. "Why you always worrying all the time?" Leroy leaned forward, and with his elbows planted on the table, he lifted the sandwich and bit into it wolfishly. He chewed and laughed shaking his head.

The bartender brought the pitcher, and Leroy slopped beer into their glasses. "To you and Kia," he said.

Marcus gripped the frosted glass and clinked it against Leroy's.

Reverend Jones loomed before the pulpit, behind Marcus, while Kia stepped down the aisle with a bouquet in her hands. Everyone in the pews watched her. She covered the bulge even though, all the way down to her fierce-eyed ten-year-old cousin, Jerome, everybody knew she was twenty-seven weeks along.

In the tux, Marcus held his chest full of air. Nancy Winslow's sobbing echoed over the organ. She'd been that way ever since Marcus had talked Kia into moving into an apartment with him.

"How will we pay for it?" Kia had asked.

"What's important," Marcus had said, "is we have a place of our own." Mostly, he hated sneaking to visit Kia. Even though Marcus had for months been Kia's fiancé, Nancy had shooed him from the house. What if the child, Marcus had thought, notices Nancy's way of treating me? What if the child absorbed Nancy's disdain?

The organ boomed while sunlight gleamed between the clouds and through stained glass windows during Kia's walk. It glared and whitened the entire church. Leroy, the best man, balanced himself beside and behind Marcus. He held the wedding ring. (When Marcus had given it to him that morning, he'd quipped, "*I do.*")

Marcus wrenched around. The tux confined Leroy's shoulders and arms. In the slacks, the prosthetic filled out like a real leg. Marcus wanted to nod at Leroy, but Leroy was squinting at the sunshine. The rays lightened his face to gold and made bold the snaking scar across his scalp. Leroy's mouth shaped itself into a questioning O.

In the basement of the church, the music played from the stereo system Marcus's mother had rented, and most of the family milled around the rectangular steel tables and wooden fold-out chairs. The three tables had plastic tablecloths over them, and his mother had arranged them in a long row, three feet apart from one another. Leroy lounged with his back to the wall and the men's room behind him, and Kia gripped Marcus's hand as they flowed towards the basement kitchen for cake cutting. Above them, children banged and shuffled in the ground floor playroom. The only other person sitting isolated at the tables was Kia's cousin Jerome.

"Get in here, Leroy," Marcus said.

"Jerome, come on," Kia called.

Marcus and Kia clasped hands and sliced through the cake. His mother took over and cut pieces for everyone.

"Where's the best man?" Marcus said. He glanced over crowding family and friends, and his father squeezed his shoulder and kissed Kia. Cheers and laughter echoed.

Across the basement floor, Leroy lumbered towards the steps to the congregation hall. To Marcus, it looked like stealth. Ten-year-old Jerome followed with his lips pursed as though he were a bruiser. Jerome, it seemed, had misunderstood Leroy's way of walking.

Marcus sank back into the crowd. His mother pushed his Grandma Abrams in a wheelchair. (The cancer had worsened, his mother had told him.) "She's so beautiful," his grandmother said, over and over, about Kia. Marcus mingled long enough to eat the cake but, as soon as he could, hurried across the basement to check on Leroy.

He mounted the steps to the ground level (voices quieting behind him) and climbed another set of steps to the children's playroom. He pushed through double doors and arrived where all eight children at the wedding were playing.

Two of them were cousins from his mother's side while another two, including the tall one flinging the frisbee, were from his father's. At the end of the room, straight ahead, stood a stage. Purple curtains hung in vertical folds on either side, and a limp American flag hung from a wooden pole. In the middle of the stage giggled two young girls, around twelve years of age. Marcus walked closer.

The taller girl, with braided hair, was Jerome's older sister, Mya, and the blond girl with the gold-rimmed glasses was the oldest child of Marcus's Aunt Kate, the older sister of his father. Both girls had doted over the two-year-old sister of the pair of boys playing frisbee. All three belonged to Marcus's uncle, who was his mother's younger brother.

Leroy bent down towards the little girl and shook her hand. He turned his face upward at Marcus when Marcus climbed the stage. The little girl had her hair in tight cornrows and wore green flower clips. Her parents had dressed her in a white, frilly dress.

"What's your name?" Leroy asked the girl.

The blond girl knelt and put one hand on the girl's shoulder. "Muneera," she said and made a stuffed frog hop for the child's enjoyment.

"What's *yours?*" Mya said.

"He Leroy," Jerome said and leapt in front of Muneera. With his legs spread apart and hands on either side of his face, he hopped from leg to leg and shook his mouth, playfully saying gibberish, until the child lifted her arms over her head and laughed.

"Are you one of our uncles?" Mya said.

"Nah," Leroy said.

At the end of the room, one of the boys banged his hands over the keys of a discordant piano. The boy stopped when Marcus's red-haired cousin announced that everyone downstairs was dancing.

All the boys scrambled from the playroom, and Jerome jockeyed to lift Muneera into his arms. The girls and Jerome moved across the playroom towards the exit.

"Come on, Leroy," Jerome called.

Soon Marcus and Leroy stood together on stage. Stuffed animals and toys cluttered the floor all around them.

"Why'd you come up here?" Marcus said. "The wine that bad?"

"It's relaxing to watch, you know?" Leroy limped from the play area, stepped over a plastic partition, and thumped over the stage's warped boards.

Marcus turned, worried, towards the exit. Voices babbled downstairs, but soon everyone would notice his absence. He stepped beside Leroy on the edge of the stage, where the air felt suddenly cool. Bulbs in the high ceiling diffused grainy, brownish-orange light.

Leroy spoke. "It ever seem to you like we still over there? Like this right here a dream we going to wake up from?" His eyelids swelled, and his lower lip sagged. He'd looked the same way during those weeks of morphine-induced silence back at the medical center.

"It does," Marcus said, "sometimes."

"We shouldn't be here. We should be there, protecting them."

"They'll be coming home soon," Marcus said.

Leroy jerked his head towards Marcus. The loose skin of his face, expressionless, jiggled. "What you mean?"

Baffled, Marcus stared until he understood: Leroy wasn't talking about marines. He wasn't even talking about Americans. He was talking about the Iraqis.

"Come on," Marcus said, "it's a wedding."

Leroy faced forward. "Yeah," he said and dug into his pocket, coming up with painkillers.

CHAPTER 6

Marcus dozed with his arm under a pillow he shared with Kia. The arm had lost circulation, numbed, and awakened him. He rolled onto his back and sat up in the hotel bed. He'd been dreaming about the sound of the water. Niagara Falls crashed down to iced-over stones. He and Kia's honeymoon suite perched forty stories over the waterfalls, and in the dream, the sound was water blasting away the hotel's foundation.

They'd gone on their honeymoon after the semester had ended so that they wouldn't miss classes, and Marcus had taken a week off work.

"Is it snowing?" Kia said, her eyelids closed.

"It is," he said. "You hungry?"

"Mm, I'm starving," she said and turned onto her back. She slipped her slender arms over the blanket.

"How're you feeling?" Late the night before, Kia had complained of pain in her stomach and had finally called her mother to ask what it meant. Her mother had asked her to come home if they got worse. Home was only three hours away.

"Better," Kia said.

Marcus rubbed his hand over her forearm. She still had an athlete's body, the runner's legs and shoulders, but her abdomen curved outward with their child.

"What's wrong?" Kia said. Marcus's hand had stilled.

"My friend's wife was going into labor when we left."

"Phil?"

"No, our sergeant." He turned towards the picture window that overlooked the falls. Snow swirled against the glass. "I'll get food," he said, "and if a café's nearby, I'll check my email to see if Leroy sent news about it."

He pecked Kia on the mouth and dressed himself for the winter evening. He kneaded a winter cap in his hands while walking from the master bedroom, and at the door, he turned to look back. The edge of the picture window reflected his image. His face was pale, his eyes hollow.

A walk of fifteen minutes brought him to the falls. He stood with his gloved hands on the guardrail. Ice slicked the railing, and below, water rushed over the bluff and crashed onto mounds of ice. He turned and walked towards the strip of restaurants and shops.

From a park, he approached the bustle of the tourist city, and the sound of the water softened behind while he trudged uphill through a stretch of open ground. Pine trees flanked him on both sides. Wet snow resisted, then gave way, and his feet sank, his legs burning from the effort. At the edge of the park, he rested his hands on his knees and coughed. He hadn't hacked like that since first returning from Baghdad, but soon he was all right, and within another minute of walking, a road appeared.

The street had shops and bars along both sides. From a store front at the corner, where cars stopped at a light, a giant Frankenstein monster lurched from the rooftop, a stationary advertisement for a haunted house. Marcus turned left at the crossroads and plunged into the flow of pedestrians. He searched for an Internet café but found none. Down the street, a restaurant window shed red neon light.

The restaurant stood on a corner where a local road sloped downhill beside it. Neon signs advertised beer. He wandered in. Baseball gloves, penants, and license plates were on the rafters. At the cashier's counter, he ordered two take-out meals of chicken fajitas. He'd have to wait twenty minutes. It was enough time, he thought, to find out about Reed's baby.

Outside, snow flakes rotated above and dizzied him. Marcus scanned the street for a café. In the balcony of the hotel across from him, two lovers howled in drunkeness. One of them, a young woman, hoisted a glass and wailed in celebration while several people on the sidewalk watched or, outraged, ignored her.

Marcus recognized someone among the onlookers.

"Sergeant Reed!" he shouted. *Could it be him? Here?*

Somewhere down the street, people began yelling. Reed quickly sank back into the crowd, with everyone moving en masse towards the commotion.

Marcus shouted again for Reed, then dashed across the street and shouldered his way into the crowd, following the movement.

"Sergeant Reed!" But it was impossible. Reed was in a hospital in Pennsylvania, about to become a father.

Still pushing through, Marcus found himself at a club entrance, where part of a crowd had gathered for a brawl. Two bouncers held a struggling man by his arms. Another man was prone on the ground. Reed was nowhere to be seen.

Soon police cruisers blared sirens and neared. Automobiles along the road stopped beside curbs to let them pass. The bouncers escorted the man towards the cruiser. As he struggled, he leapt into the air only to be yanked back to earth.

The police cuffed the man and threw him into the back seat. The man immediately bashed his head against the passenger side window, his skull slightly bowing the reinforced glass outwards. Seemingly dazed, he shouted at the crowd while young men pointed and mocked.

Marcus pushed his way back to the main road and returned to the restaurant. It was quiet inside.

His food was ready, so he paid the cashier and glanced up at a muted television behind her. The television showed a murderer in the United States being apprehended. The killer's picture flashed over the screen. Marcus looked around for someone to tell, but he was alone. The man on television was Mike.

That night Marcus dreamed he found Sergeant Reed in the bathroom of the honeymoon suite. Dressed in the desert fatigue pants, a shirtless Reed perched on the edge of the jacuzzi bath and gripped the Marine-issued Ka-Bar fighting knife blade-down.

Reed inspected his leg then, holding the fabric of the pants taut, ran the black blade straight down his thigh, shredding the cloth from kneecap to pelvis, then dropped the knife into the sink.

"Shh," Marcus said. Kia slept in the next room.

Reed tore the pantleg open. "You see, Private?" Reed said, his whole body poised over the gangrenous tissue.

"Shut up," Marcus said. "Quiet."

By Marcus and Kia's third morning, the sound of the falls had stopped, and everything silenced. The waterfalls had frozen through, and the cataracts resembled smooth-feathered backs of cascading angels.

Around five in the morning, Kia came from the bathroom and stumbled to the side of the bed. She switched on the nightstand lamp, and Marcus squinted. Kia's face was ashen, with bags beneath her eyes. Behind her in the bathroom, the toilet tank refilled with water.

"We have to go," she said and fell back onto the bed.

Marcus fumbled at the phone and alerted the man at the front desk to ready the Subaru. He helped Kia put on sweatpants, socks, and shoes, and after he'd scrambled through the hotel room once for anything important they'd left unpacked, he tugged both suitcases behind him as they hurried down the hallway towards the elevator.

Marcus and a hotel staff member propped Kia up. They trudged through the snow towards the car while flakes whirled against their faces. Kia sat down in the passenger seat and blew into her cupped hands. Soon Marcus jumped in and directed all heating vents towards her. He adjusted the seat and, driving, shifted only as high as second gear while they moved down the hotel service road, through the unpeopled downtown strip, and across Peace Bridge to America.

Back on the highway, he plowed through the snowy roads. In some stretches, the Subaru drove through inches of unbroken white.

"They're getting worse," Kia said. "In my legs now."

He wanted to speed but might lose control.

They arrived at a mile of road where the snow had eased up, and where the overcast sky cleaved open almost to the sun. The clouds shifted apart, trailing wisps like fibers of cotton, and Marcus shifted into fifth gear. He hunched his shoulders and accelerated.

He manuevered around gentle turns and had the car up to eighty miles per hour when the snow stopped altogether.

The lucidity of the blue that loomed above astonished him. In his life, the sky had never shone that way before. It was a cut in the body of the universe.

They made it only as far as Buffalo. Marcus sat in the hospital chair until sweat dampened the seat cushion, and Kia lay before him with black straps of the fetal monitor around her abdomen. The nurses had adjusted her birthing bed enough for her to sit up.

When a nurse named Alexandria (Alex, she insisted they call her) made Kia walk around to relax her body, wrinkles formed on Kia's forehead and on the bridge of her nose, and her upper lip lifted and revealed her teeth and gums. Alex had been with them since the hospital admitted Kia at seven in the morning, and the nurse had the habit of making everyone around her nervous by rushing, almost on the brink of confusion, through every action. She had black hair cut short and pulled back behind her head, where a red elastic band clamped the hair in place. With her airy blue eyes and a face that narrowed to the tip of her nose, Nurse Alex looked to Marcus (who wanted her to calm the hell down) like a startled albino mouse.

During the twelfth hour, Marcus isolated himself in the chilly stairwell at the end of the hall. He hugged his stomach because something he'd eaten was cutting him up.

Another expectant father had been smoking a cigarette in the stairwell and had hidden it behind his back when Marcus pushed open the door. The man wore slacks and a shirt open around the collar. Over his undershirt hung a cross on a chain.

The man stood half a flight of stairs below Marcus, facing out the narrow window in the brick wall. The window overlooked the parking lot, where cars stood covered in snow, and further out, the city skyline appeared through falling flakes. Through the window, the edges of the taller buildings emerged from the snowfall like black tankers back home sometimes emerged from heavy fog. The man turned and walked up the steps, and keys jangled in his slacks pocket. He was a banker, Marcus thought, or a school superintendant.

"You look like you need a cigarette," the man said.

"No, thanks," Marcus replied.

The man reached into his pocket, and Marcus heard the keys again. "If you change your mind, I left one between a couple bricks down by the window."

The man left behind a scent of cologne.

While Marcus was waiting in the cold air of the stairwell, a newborn baby cried. Marcus ran to the reinforced window in the door when the cologne-scented man, dressed in blue scrubs, with a mask dangling around his neck, jumped into the hallway as if searching for someone to tell. The hallway narrowed from the stairwell to the brightly lit waiting room. The man bounded towards the stairs but halted. He lifted his face towards the reinforced glass window and returned to the birthing room. Marcus wondered if perhaps a nurse or doctor had told him Marcus had been haunting that floor for a long time.

Kia shrieked and Marcus burst from the stairwell. Nurse Alex stopped him. She was wearing gloves.

"Please stay in the waiting room where we can find you this time, Mister Green, and we'll call you back shortly."

"What's happening?"

"We'll call you back shortly. Everything's going to be fine."

So Marcus started down the hall towards the waiting room. There, nurses talked with patients without making eye contact, looking at computer screens and punching buttons on keyboards. At seven in the evening, the waiting room smelled of antiseptic, and the seats reminded him of seats in airport terminals, rows of soft-cushioned, imitation leather chairs. The rows surrounded coffee tables that were large rectangular blocks, tables without legs, weighed down with wrinkled *Time* magazines and comforting pamphlets about dealing with cancer. One wide window formed the far wall, and several rows of chairs faced the snow-obliterated city. Nobody could come to Buffalo from Ashtabula in this, he knew. He'd tried to call Kia's mother, but Nancy hadn't been home. And he'd lied when he told Kia he tried to call his own parents. For now, he felt better off alone. He sat in front of the window, with fake ferns and violets on top of a bookshelf beneath the glass. A few seats over, a long-haired man leaned forward, resting his forehead against a Bible. The man's hair fell forward and hid his face. Marcus leaned back and watched the window shake from the blizzard. "Everything's going to be fine," the nurse had said.

The baby was breech. They put Marcus in blue scrubs and a mask at two o'clock in the morning and took him to Kia for the Cesarean. He stood on Kia's right side, and the nurse pulled a white curtain across Kia's chest to hide her stomach. Marcus held Kia's hand.

"Did you call Mama?" she said.

"She's snowed in," he said, "but she said she's praying."

The doctor was doing something to Kia. The bed rail Marcus leaned against shook.

"It hurts," she said. Her eyelids twitched, and sweat beaded on her lip.

Marcus had his face inches from hers. The curtain hid it all. They were cutting her.

"Pulling," she said and leaned her head back, deeper into the pillows.

A machine behind the curtain made a suction noise. Nurse Alex had said they would have to do that to clean the baby's nose and mouth. Marcus kept his gaze locked on Kia's face. She was trying to look around him, and he moved his head to block her view. He wanted her to stay with him.

"Marcus," she said, "why isn't it crying?"

"Shh," he said. He kept his face close to hers and repeated, without knowing what his words meant, "It's all right. It's all all right." He had also expected the child to cry. He could look, but he was afraid.

All at once, the child did cry. Kia blushed, and her eyes moved in jerks. Marcus turned to look past the curtain.

The baby, eyelids shut tight, wailed. The wailing vibrated in Marcus's chest cavity.

Marcus pressed against the birthing bed's side rail, and Kia reclined on the pillows. The curtain covered the wound across her midsection. She turned her head towards Marcus and smiled while the child cried triumphantly in the next room.

"Is it a girl?" she said, and Marcus smelled the bicitra on her breath.

"A boy," Marcus said. Before the nurses had dashed away, they'd shown Marcus the child. In spite of everything it looked healthy—perhaps he hadn't hurt it. Marcus couldn't help remembering Kia had wanted to give birth naturally, and that she'd hoped for a girl.

"I'm sorry."

"Why?" Marcus said. "You were a champion."

Nurse Alex wore a mask and goggles. She touched Marcus's elbow. "Mister Green, we need you to wait in the next room."

"What's wrong?"

"It's a delicate procedure. Please—"

Marcus jerked his head back to Kia, but she was already dozing under the anesthesia. He let Nurse Alex draw him away.

The florescent lights in the private waiting room buzzed in the ceiling as he leaned forward in the seat. Another row of seats, all bolted together and grounded, stretched across from him. A single window faced the iced-over city. The long, narrow waiting room had a door at both ends. The doors had glass rectangles over the knobs. He watched for someone to enter.

On the wall in front of Marcus hung a watercolor framed with cherry wood. A woman with coal-smudged skin, dressed in a crimson dress, perched on a park bench. Behind the woman, a garden overflowed with blossoms. The woman held an umbrella over an old-fashioned baby buggy, and her knees showed from under the hem of the dress. The kneecaps, round and smooth, looked like the crowns of baby skulls.

Someone came in from the operating room. It was the gaunt doctor, and Marcus was sure that either Kia or the baby had died. The man stepped to Marcus's side and reached out a milky hand.

"I'm Edgar Cunningham," he said. The doctor bent his ancient knees and sat down across from Marcus.

"What's wrong?"

"No, nothing's wrong." The doctor's hand shot up to his face. He itched his high forehead. "You can see your wife shortly. As for your boy—" The doctor leaned forward with his elbows on his thighs. He interlocked his hands in front of his mouth as though praying.

"What is it?" Marcus said, but he knew. There was a defect. What had choked him in the Al-Salaam district had harmed his child.

"You can see your son immediately."

A rush of air cooled Marcus's face when the doctor walked past and out the door. Marcus breathed shallowly and walked to the other end of the waiting room, to the glass door that looked out into the larger waiting area. The boy, was there really nothing wrong? Marcus turned and faced the narrow length of the room.

Marcus and Kia's wailing child had made the hospital floor tremble. In front of him, on the wall, the thick-boned woman in the watercolor protected the child in the baby buggy by wielding the umbrella. Marcus realized why the painting intrigued him. The woman in the painting resembled his mother.

The old doctor and Nurse Alex lined up outside the glass door. The doctor held the door open for the nurse, who cradled their son. A blanket made a cotton nest around the child. Nurse Alex said something that Marcus missed as she crouched down and presented Marcus his son, and Marcus snuggled the bundle to his chest.

The child smelled like honey. His eyes squinted closed, but when they opened, blue-green irises flashed.

"Eight pounds," Nurse Alex said. Tufts of curly hair sprouted from the child's head.

"Mister Green," Doctor Cunningham said. He'd gone away and come back. He held the door open. "Your wife's ready."

Marcus walked past the doctor, the child against his chest. After he entered Kia's room, Nurse Alex passed him to prepare a spot for the baby under Kia's arm.

Kia asked where her son was, and Nurse Alex said Marcus was coming right then. "Ooh," Kia said, and her mouth pursed into a pained coo. Nurse Alex had folded a blanket beneath Kia's arm so that she could comfort the baby without the baby's weight causing her pain. Marcus laid the child beside her, and the boy's head of black, angelic curls rested on her shoulder.

Kia reached over with delicate fingers and worried the boy's blanket. The child's eyelids opened, and blue-green irises flashed again.

"Like my father's," Marcus said.

CHAPTER 7

At four thirty in the morning, the alarm clock woke Marcus, who lay on the bedroom floor beside Kia's bed. In the night, Benjamin Marco Green, two weeks old, sprawled out, so Marcus rolled away, afraid of turning over on the child.

His lower back pinched as he staggered to his feet. In the dark, he rubbed his bare arms with his hands. He'd lain on the floor in boxer shorts only and grown cold.

The floor creaked beneath his feet as he tiptoed from the room and down the hallway to the bathroom. He reached the cool floor tiles, flipped the light switch, and swayed over the toilet bowl, his eyes adjusting. On the outside of the bathroom window, ice from freezing rain clung like a cataract.

Once he'd returned to the bedroom, he leaned over Benjamin and sniffed around the boy's diaper—a faint apple smell. He kissed the boy with a peck and scooped him up, and he murmured pressing lips to Ben's forehead. "Everything's all right." Ben squirmed but calmed when Marcus laid him on a blanket in the living room, a known routine.

Ever since returning from Buffalo with their son, Kia had stayed at her mother's house, and Marcus had stayed with her. On the fold-out kitchen table of their one-room apartment in Ashtabula Harbor (more an idea than a home, and now forgotten), a warning of eviction glared in bold black letters, but that concerned him as little as Nancy's silence. He kissed Benjamin's belly, and the boy clamped his arms on Marcus's face.

The phone rang, so Marcus cradled the boy with one arm, slid onto the couch, and answered. It was his mother. Her voice careened in strained tones. "Marcus," she said, "your Grandma Abrams is unwell, but she won't take hospice help no more." There was a long pause, and when his mother spoke again, she asked if he and Kia could come over with the baby. His grandmother still hadn't seen Ben Marco.

"We'll be right over," he said.

When Marcus brought Ben, dry and powdered, back to the bed, Kia was sitting up.

"You going to work?" she said and looked with sleepy eyes at Benjamin, still cradled in Marcus's arms.

The morning sky swirled with snow while Marcus drove the car through unplowed roads. Benjamin wore a child's winter cap and faced the icy back window from the car seat, and Kia hugged her legs to her chest.

Marcus parked outside his grandmother's house and ran around the car's front end to help unbelt Benjamin. With the carseat hooked under his arm, flakes stinging his face, he walked through the blowing snow up the walkway. Kia knocked.

Marcus's mother had been watching from the front door, and she unburdened Marcus, taking Benjamin the moment they entered. She gave the child to Kia after she'd slipped off her boots, coat, hat, and gloves. A bitter, earthy scent lingered heavily, and as Marcus and Kia walked through the plant-filled living room and towards the master bedroom, the smell sharpened.

His grandmother's bed looked elevated. In it, she snored using an oxygen nose tube. Marcus's mother stood on the opposite side of the bed, her arms crossed over her stomach.

"Mama?" his mother said.

His grandmother opened her mouth and eyes as though awakening from a troubling dream, and as her mouth closed, she folded her hands one on top of the other, wheezing quietly.

"Grandma," Marcus said. "This is Benjamin Marco Green. He's your great-grandson."

Kia stepped closer and eased herself onto the bed, the child slumbering in her arms, and Grandma Abrams nodded and pressed her lips tight as though to speak, but her eyes rolled to one side, and she stilled herself.

From the other side of the bed, his mother watched. She rubbed her nose with her palm and squeezed the fabric of her sweater.

"This was what she wanted," she said. "She kept asking to see."

Stacks of photographs formed a mound on the nightstand, and Marcus noticed a dozen boxes cluttering the room. Boxes of photographs also lined the wall and the foot of the bed.

"What're these pictures doing out?"

"We looked together," his mother said.

Marcus picked a photograph off the top of one pile at the corner of the nightstand. It was his great-grandfather Abrams in an army uniform, and someone had penciled *1918* on the back of the yellowed paper.

"I've never seen these before," Marcus said.

The next photograph showed a burly, bearded man who, while he tucked one hand into his suit coat, gripped a rifle in the other.

"They're yours," his mother said. "Mama wants you to have them."

The back of the second photo read *Chicago, 1919*. He flipped the photograph over again and noticed, behind the beard, his great-grandfather's broad forehead and weary eyes.

Marcus replaced the photos and stood against Kia, who cradled the child on the bedside for his grandmother to see. He gripped his wife's shoulder, and his grandmother's eyes quivered.

Marcus sensed an audience. With the light in the room grainy orange, the color of dreamlight, he imagined people standing all around him. They were kinfolk, a hundred faces with shared lines, who'd helped Benjamin come along.

The next morning, Marcus woke with the alarm clock and carried Benjamin into the living room to change him. Afterwards he clicked off the lamplight and sat in the dark. Outside, a foot of snow layered the backyard and weighed down pine limbs.

The day before, Marcus, Kia, and Benjamin had stayed well into the afternoon, and Marcus had forgotten to call Gayle at work. He'd thought of it, had known he ought to, but had finally called too late, after Gayle had left, and only left a message with a cashier. All that had mattered was his grandmother. That evening, with Marcus's mother the only one in the house, his Grandma Abrams passed away.

Once again, Kia was sitting up in the bed when he walked in cradling Benjamin. She asked if he was going to work.

"If Gayle takes me back," he said. He laid Ben down and slid out his hands. Then he sat down on the bed. "You going to school?" he asked softly. He'd asked the same question during the drive from Buffalo to Ashtabula. Then, she'd wanted to suspend her schoolwork, at least for Benjamin's earliest months.

"I can't," she said. "Don't want to leave him."

Across the hall, Nancy yanked open her bedroom door. Her bedroom lamp shed reddish light.

"You going to school?" Nancy demanded, peering at Marcus. Marcus looked at Benjamin.

"I don't *know*," Kia mumbled.

"And what about you?" Nancy asked Marcus.

"You know he's got to work," Kia said.

Nancy pointed a finger. "And you've got to go to school."

"Mama," Kia said, and she dabbed her midsection with her fingertips. "I told you yesterday—" She turned her head and pushed her face into the pillow, and her body closed more snugly around Ben.

"She can't go," Marcus said.

"Yes, she can," Nancy said. "Don't tell me she can't. She can switch to night classes anytime she want." Nancy came close and lifted a finger in front of his face. "My daughter," she said, lifting her chin, "was valedictorian."

Marcus parked across from the gasoline pumps at ten minutes before six. He stomped through the snow-covered walkway but halted. By the main doors, bloody snow covered a shovel. Marcus picked it up and, after dodging an exiting man, shuffled inside.

The trail of blood led to a booth beside the food court. Gayle stood over an old man who held a rag to the back of his head. Truckers used the rags when they showered in the back. The new maintenance man had apparently tossed away a few shovelfuls of snow then slipped and split his scalp on the ice. Gayle had over-blushed her bony cheeks, and her grim lips pressed together.

"You didn't call yesterday," she said as if his reappearance bored her. "Andy's our morning man now."

Andy was over seventy and leaned with both elbows on the tabletop. His hair was combed back in an old-fashioned slick, and as he leaned forward, bearing the wound, drool trickled from his opened lips.

Marcus tried to explain, but Gayle wouldn't listen, so he unsnapped the vest, slid it off his shoulders, and handed it to her. He turned back towards the front doors, where a hoard of truckers and other people gassing up before work mumbled around the cash registers. The only cashier in the station was fiddling outside by the gas pumps with an automatic receipt dispenser.

"Marcus," Gayle said.

As she flew towards the cash register, she threw him back his ridiculous vest.

Marcus used a dolly to lug a barrel of salt around the truck stop. Gayle had directed him to de-ice the walkway around the store, as well as the gasoline and diesel pumps. It was ten thirty in the morning, and salt burned his hands even though he wore plastic gloves beneath leather ones.

He shuffled backwards, pulling the dolly through the slush, and scooped handfuls of salt that he scattered. The snow closest to him fizzed, pockmarked, while the snow farther behind grayed, melting off the cement.

After he'd finished, he shoved the dolly against the back wall and squatted on the curb. In front of him, the lot stretched for fifty feet, and beyond the asphalt, the ground sloped and leveled off at a field of cornstalks and clumps of frozen mud. The field ended after a quarter mile, where leafless hardwoods swayed.

A semi rumbled around the side and passed him, spewing the metal stench of spent diesel, and parked with its trailer towards the field. Marcus, his knees up at chest level, rested his arms on his thighs, and when snow dripped off his cap and caught on his eyelashes, he rubbed it in with the back of his hand. Instantly salt residue burned. He rolled over holding his face, then ran across the lot towards the field.

At the edge of the lot, he skidded down the slope and crashed into icy clumps. He flung off his gloves and pressed his face into snow until it numbed. He spat into the slush, got to his feet, and climbed the rise back to the lot. Another semi lumbered around the edge of the storefront and churned towards him, spattering up slush. It blared its horn, and Marcus trotted out of its way.

But on the sidewalk, he paused. By the back door, a mass of fur hulked. It was Leroy, advancing in a black coat and Russian-style cap.

"You trying to kill yourself?"

"Never," Marcus said. They shook hands and pressed shoulders.

"Good, because I'm here to recruit you."

After work, Marcus drove towards The Anchor. He pulled into the slushy parking lot at twenty minutes after two and parked behind the black Cadillac Leroy had rented and driven from Cleveland. What the hell kind of work was Leroy doing, Marcus wondered, to have the money for a Cadillac, even if it was a rental? Those furs had to have cost something too. Probably they were imitation.

Bells jingled when Marcus pushed open the door. As always, anchors decorated the wallpaper, and the real anchor leaned behind the bar, a leftover Christmas bow on it. Leroy sat with his back to a corner. It was the same seat Marcus had sat in before the wedding.

As soon as Marcus sat, the waitress brought two frosted glasses of beer.

"Congratulations," Leroy said. He hoisted the glass and leaned forward.

"Thank you," Marcus said.

They drank, the beer foaming down Marcus's throat. Ice clung to the window beside him.

"Now," Leroy said, "what you going to do?"

"Kia's taking time off from school to stay with the baby, and next year I'll—"

"Nah," Leroy said. He waved his hand. "Listen. Squirrel didn't have your luck."

Leroy dug a thumbnail into the table before he gulped from the glass, nearly emptying it, and then, leaning forward, he told Marcus that there'd been a deformity. He withheld the details.

"So what I mean," Leroy said, "is what you going to *do*?"

"Take care of my own," he said.

Leroy tilted his head and stared, and his eyes blurred over. "When I helped form this group, and we took that van to L.A., it was just half a dozen of us brittle vets. Broke and hungry. We had the rally, and we realized it's homeless people all over the city, and most of them vets. They was staggering round us on our march. Some of them drunk, yes, but with us. Now we got two busloads all riding across the country. It's growing."

"What do you want?"

"We're going to Kent State tomorrow, and in two days, we're going to D.C." Leroy wrapped his hand around his beer. "I want you to join up."

"But I've got Kia," Marcus said. "I've got my boy."

"Who's your family?" Leroy said. "Where's it end? We've got families like yours, and we've got families like Squirrel's. Ain't no difference. We all came through the same stuff and luck made us this way."

Marcus shut his eyes. The talk about family made him recall the photographs beside his grandmother's deathbed. At the same time, ice peeled back off the window and crashed, breaking on the sidewalk.

His grandmother's funeral was in two days.

"I have to think," Marcus said.

CHAPTER 8

Puddles of slush had formed in the road. The road wound through fields, and along either side stood century-old frame houses, silos, and sagging barns.

"Benjamin," Marcus said, "alone with Grandma at last."

"You're going to quit your job?" Kia said.

"I didn't say that." What he'd said was Leroy wanted them, after the funeral the next day, to drive to D.C. Marcus would have to miss work, and Gayle might not take him back.

Kia wrapped her arms around her waist. "I didn't want to go back to that apartment anyway," she said. "So cold."

A half hour later, he pulled the crimson Subaru into the university driveway, the library in front of him, and headed towards the visitor parking lot. Two buses idled, the bottom feet of their rectangular exteriors covered with salt residue and black ice, and behind them jutted the kiva auditorium attached to the six-acre plaza and student center complex. A dozen people smoked cigarettes, milling in front of the glass wall and doors of the lobby, their shoulders raised to fight off the cold.

Marcus stopped at the security gate and took a parking permit from an automated dispenser. The gate lifted, and the car slogged through the slushy lot. Almost as soon as he parked, heavy sheets of sleet slammed down.

Kia leaned forward, her arms still wrapped around her waist.

"What exactly are we doing here?" she said.

"Leroy's organization is passing through," he said. "Let's just see what they're about."

"But why'd you want me here?" she said.

"Because," he said, "Leroy wants our support, and I want yours."

Leroy, Marcus knew, wanted more. In D.C., Leroy's group of vets would be demonstrating during the presidential inauguration.

"I'm not walking through this," she said, "but I should call Mama."

"Then let's run for it." He dug into junk collected under the backseat and found a beat up umbrella. Kia squealed that it didn't even work.

"Of course it does," he said. "Watch." He flung open the door, and sleet pelted him as he turned around, hunching forward to fumble with the umbrella. Finally he got the thing open, and he closed the car door and strolled back and forth in front of the car as though it were sprinkling.

Kia smiled and shook her head, and Marcus came to her side of the car and knocked on the window.

After she popped her coat collar, she stepped from the car. "Crazy man," she said and hooted at the sleet.

They walked together and approached the edge of the student center plaza and kiva lobby, and the group of smokers opened up as if to receive them. Several men wore desert camo fatigue jackets. Before he and Kia reached the main doors, Kia stopped.

"What is it?" he said.

She leaned in as if to kiss him but instead snatched the umbrella. "I'm calling Mama," she said, "in private."

Marcus stepped into the lobby where unknown people stood on both sides. Kia reached the student center doors. When he turned around and faced opened doors to the underground hall, people dressed in blazers, sports coats, or jackets of the desert camo uniform shifted like walls of water. They waved Styrofoam cups in front of their chins and spoke, and beside him, a gaunt man in a blazer filled a cup with coffee from a large, square thermos. He blew over the surface of his drink and raised wisps of steam. Something about the man reminded Marcus of Doctor Cunningham from Buffalo.

Marcus went over to the table and poured himself a cup of thin convention brew, and he sipped it waiting for Kia to return. When she did, he handed her a cup of coffee, and they made their way into the downward slanting kiva, where people gathered in isolated groups or pairs. He and Kia sat in the far right side. Down near the stage, Leroy wore a constricting blazer and stood in the pit area. Behind him, the narrow, wooden podium showed the university's blue and gold seal. The podium reminded Marcus of a child's casket.

When most of the people had found a seat, Leroy used the metal railing and mounted the three steps to the stage. He then swaggered to the podium, adjusted the microphone, and asked anyone still in the lobby to please find a seat. After another pause, he thanked everyone for coming and introduced the first speaker, a man whose legs shook as he climbed the stage. The man had the thin, stretched skin on his face that grew after burns healed, pink blotches on his chin and lips. He leaned over the podium and inhaled, his voice raspy.

"I went to Kuwait and then we launched the bombs, and in we stormed." The speaker stopped to gather himself. He wore a short-sleeved shirt that exposed a forearm-to-hand prosthetic. After he breathed in deeply, he described an incident in which his company had strapped insurgents to the hood of a Humvee. He said one captive's brain had cooked on the grill. "Why'd we do that?" he asked. "There's no such thing as self-sufficiency. At the end of the day, we depended on them for food and water, for supplies. What does that make us?"

It was true, Marcus thought. Hurting the Iraqis was hurting themselves, self-mutilation, and that's why being injured by one of them was like being injured by a family member.

"I need the restroom," Kia said, already standing up.

"You all right?" he said.

"Be back," she said.

He stood to let her pass, and for all he could tell, for the rest of the speech she never came back. The door at the back of the kiva creaked open, and perhaps she'd taken a seat near the back to keep from making a disruption.

After the veteran had told his story, Leroy lumbered to the stage once more and thanked everyone for coming. "We'll be in D.C. beginning tomorrow," Leroy said. "Thank you." As soon as Leroy concluded the forum, some members of the audience burst into claps while others bolted towards the exit.

Leroy shook hands with the same gaunt-faced man who looked like Doctor Cunningham. He gestured as they spoke, eyes opened wide. After some time, the man and Leroy walked up the aisle, and Leroy lifted his arm in Marcus's direction.

"Marcus," Leroy said, his voice hoarse, "this is Professor Corner from Middle Eastern Studies." Marcus, the umbrella in his left fist, shook the man's thin-bone hand. "Marcus and I," Leroy said, "were in the same unit together in Baghdad." The professor, his head cocked, nodded and pursed his lips.

"Interesting," the professor said.

They made their way through the people to get coffee, Leroy leading and the professor in the rear. Marcus searched for Kia but thought she might've gone back to the student center to check up on Ben Marco again. After he filled the Styrofoam cup, he, Leroy, and the professor formed a triangle for conversation.

"Kia met Nurse Sheila," Leroy said, glancing at Marcus and pointing across the room.

Kia spoke confidentially with a young woman who had a red and blue handkerchief clamped around a bundle of bleached dreadlocks.

"May I ask how long you've been back?" the professor said. He had almost colorless blue eyes, and his breath stunk of chewed cigar stubs.

"A little under a year," Marcus said. Kia and Sheila both turned their heads towards him, so Marcus lifted the hand with the cup to wave. Sheila smiled, her cheeks deep with dimples, her eyes weary. He sipped from the cup, but the coffee had cooled to lukewarm in the large brown thermos.

"You should accompany us—to the vigil," the professor said.

"Professor Corner's a board member at the peace center," Leroy said, chewing a cookie.

"I don't know. This is the first time we've left the baby."

"With this weather," Leroy said to Professor Corner, "we might start towards D.C. tonight. Might have to postpone the vigil."

"I suppose it might clear up tomorrow," the professor said, "at least in this region of Ohio."

"Same in D.C.," Leroy said, "but won't stay clear for long, not this winter."

"Is that Squirrel?" Marcus said.

"You said you have a child," the professor said. "Leroy tells me it's all right. You're lucky."

"I know," Marcus said. The professor's bony face seemed to hover, detached, beside him.

"It's a tragic truth civilians must also bear," the professor said.

Marcus clenched his fist, wanting to ask "What the fuck do you know?" but said nothing. Sheila, wearing a white sweater turtleneck, took her baby into her arms.

"Sergeant Squirrel," Leroy shouted, "Private Marcus Green." Leroy lifted an arm and pointed down at Marcus.

"When're you going to speak for us?" Professor Corner said.

Marcus heard but understood nothing because Kia turned from Squirrel's child and gaped her mouth in realization. The infant Sheila held, wrapped in a violet blanket, stretched out its arms and yawned. Even from across the room, when the light caught the flash of pink skin where the baby's eyes should've been, Marcus understood. Like the boy whose father had detonated himself beside Marcus and Leroy, this child was blind.

That night, Marcus had a nightmare concerning his father. In the dream, his father burst into the room Marcus shared with Kia and Ben Marco, and he aimed a pistol at Marcus, and Marcus knew his father was going to kill him. It was revenge for Marcus finding Oscar. When Samuel fired, the round entered Marcus's skull in a flash of pressure. Cloudy silence followed, but he lived. His father aimed again to finish it. To save himself, Marcus said aloud, "Samuel Green did it; Samuel Green shot and killed his son, Marcus," as though reading the headlines of a newspaper. The dream ended with his father standing over him, dangling the pistol in his hand over Marcus's face. The barrel moved in a circle around his mouth and nose.

When Marcus woke, Ben was stirring.

Ben felt heavier than usual. "Shh," Marcus said, "let's get you dry." He held the child against his chest and walked across the carpet. After he entered the living room, he spread out the blanket, laid Ben in the middle of it, and changed him.

Afterwards, Ben reached out his arms. It was his way of calming down, so Marcus placed his face close enough to the baby's bare chest to feel its warmth. The child's fingers clasped Marcus's face, the smooth right cheek and the rough skin of the scarred one.

For several minutes, Marcus knelt over Ben, and all at once he panicked.

How could he do right by Ben Marco? His will alone seemed feeble, and he felt in awe of Benjamin. A parent was fragile while a child had leveling power.

He lifted Ben, flipped off the lamplight, and tiptoed back to bed.

CHAPTER 9

The burial happened on the clearest day that winter. The sun glared off frosted grass. Everyone in the family who'd celebrated Marcus and Kia's marriage stood around his Grandma Abrams's suspended casket. A tarp housed the box and the open plot, and around Marcus were all the tombstones of his family.

Reverend Byron Jones cupped an open Bible in one hand and spoke before the grave. Flowers rustled, and the wind blew cold. It was sunny but still winter. Marcus's feet had numbed, and his fingers ached. His mother squeezed his hand and held a tissue to her face. She wore a heavy fur hat and black coat, and next to her, Kia wrapped her arms around her body. Behind Marcus and his immediate family, other family members and friends shifted from leg to leg, staying warm and listening. The sunshine blinded him but gave no warmth. The wind whipped around his head, making his ear hurt.

At the edge of the graveyard, a black mass hunched against a tree. Leroy had come in the rented Cadillac. He wore the fur coat and hat, gloves on his hands, and stamped the ground to stay warm. He stood in black frozen mud.

Bill Norman and his wife were babysitting Ben Marco. Marcus had asked his father first, but his father had wanted to attend the burial.

"The dear soul," his father had said, "she attended Dad's funeral last year."

So Marcus had phoned Mister Norman, who had solemnly agreed to watch his son.

"And you've got an audience," Bill Norman had said, "at the school whenever you want it."

Reverend Byron Jones concluded the burial. " 'And our hope in you is steadfast, knowing that as we are partakers of the sufferings,'" the reverend said, clamping closed the Bible, " 'so shall we be also of the consolation.'"

Leroy also wanted to give Marcus an audience, and to that audience Marcus knew what he'd say.

That night, after the funeral, Marcus's father phoned to ask for help. A semi, his father said, had violently smeared a family of deer over the road. The driver had fled the scene, and his father asked Marcus to drive over and help clear away the mess.

As Marcus drove towards Orwell, snow wisped slantwise across the road. It swirled and shifted like ghostly waves. Because of the storm, the headlights cast light on nothing but currents of drifting snow directly ahead, so Marcus gripped the wheel and drove with discipline. The snow caressed him towards the ditch. In Baghdad, sand had blown past roads that way, but the sun back there had blinded him while, now, he leaned towards the windshield and focused on the snow-covered road.

In Orwell, he plowed down his father's driveway. The Ford pickup's headlights were on, and a cloud of exhaust billowed from the tailpipe and expanded gray-white. A shadow sat behind the wheel. Marcus parked beside the gasoline cistern, shut off the engine, and tugged on a winter cap before stepping from the car into a half-foot of unbroken white. He crunched over to the truck. His father's tools were in the truck bed: rope, chainsaw, shovels, and lime. His father had placed four cinderblocks over the rear axle because the weight helped tires grip slippery road. Marcus opened the passenger side door, said, "Nice night," and slid in.

His father handed him a thermos of coffee. "Thanks for coming," he said, and he told Marcus where the deer lay. He and Bill Norman would chug the tractor with the front-end loader over the next morning, so all he and Marcus needed to do that night was heave the carcasses into the truck bed, shovel snow and lime over the dead meat, and go back to the farm, leaving the deer there until morning. The last thing his father wanted was to leave a smorgasbord for starving coyotes or worse (rumors had been spreading) wolves.

Bare trees formed walls on both sides of the road. The wisps of snow scattered from left to right, and flakes retreated across the windshield as Marcus and his father channeled towards the dead animals. The crack in the windshield had, as Marcus predicted, pitchforked into the dash by winter. Marcus would hardly have been able to see on a clear night.

"Radio?" his father asked.

"No thanks," Marcus said. He was wondering why the truck driver never stopped, just plowed through and never called anybody. The deer would've even caused damage to a semi, so the driver would have to stop eventually.

All at once, to Marcus, the reason seemed simple. The driver had sped off to make good time, uncaring of the mess strewn behind. It was selfishness, a desire to answer to nobody.

Marcus wondered if that same impulse lurked in him. Was that why the old Russian man had lived alone in the shack? Or why the peasant, back in Mexico, had lived amid books in the trees?

And what about his father? *He chose me over Oscar. Why? Because it was easier?*

"Do you miss Oscar?" Marcus said.

His father's hands tightened over the steering wheel. The leather gloves crackled, the material drawn taut over his knuckles. "The thing is, I never knew about him," his father said.

"She was beautiful," Marcus said, and he couldn't wholly blame his father for going with Rosita to the bedroom. The body's selfish, he thought.

"But why'd you leave Rosita the first time?" Marcus said.

They collided with snow, moving down the road, for a long time. Finally his father sniffled, then huffed a laugh as if embarrassed. "Never bawled so hard in my life," he said, "than I did on that bus to the airport." His father slowed. Red traffic lights at the intersection blinked.

So it hadn't been easy. His father hadn't wanted to stay in America. So why did he?

"Almost there," his father said.

The answer was obvious and unsettling. Love for an unborn child formed through expectation. His father had never known about Oscar, but he'd known Marcus would be born.

The Ford pickup stopped at the intersection. Snow tumbled over the windshield, and flakes, falling on the hood, melted.

Marcus identified a troubling feeling, a feeling he'd felt, he now realized, when they'd given him the Purple Heart, the same feeling he'd had last night during the dream in which his father buried a bullet in Marcus's skull. Whether I like it or not, he thought, this is who I am, this man who is broken and yet still whole. *I'm what they say I am, but also something else.*

To Leroy's audience in D.C., this was what he'd say: family happened partly by accident, included, every time, the unwanted, the uncontrollable. It was the same in Iraq, Marcus would say. Leroy was right about the Corps. Marcus had been wrong in expecting they'd make anything but wreckage. We make what we are, Marcus would say, and since we made our enemies that way, and they made us this way, we are they. *We're all of us family by accident.*

"We're here," his father said, and he and Marcus stepped from the truck, snow swirling all around them, clinging to eyelashes, to gather dead deer.

As Marcus drove along the freeway, he wore his winter coat and cap. The heater puffed warm air and made his eyes itch. It was almost midnight when they crossed the Potomac into Virginia and moved along the water until, at last, they again crossed the river into the capital.

They moved with the D.C. traffic. American flags unfurled in the snowy wind in every direction, hanging from bridges, posts, and streetlights for the presidential inauguration the following day. Graffiti on brick walls replaced hanging flags as he crept northward to the youth hostel. The hostel stood at the end of a connected line of storefronts, its parking lot beside it. In a white booth with an exposed bulb above, the parking lot monitor slouched on a stool reading a book.

"It looks like a church," Kia said, leaning forward.

Hostel windows overlooked the parking lot. Some of the lodgers had their lights turned on, but most of the panes of glass reflected the night sky and streetlights. Gusts of wind blew along the wall, and another building turned the wind inward to create a whirl. The wind that blew across the lot hit Marcus slanting upwards. Kia tucked the blanket around Ben's face.

As they walked into the narrow lobby on the ground floor, old and torn chairs stood on either side of them. Foam swelled from the imitation leather. The clerk at the front desk spoke over the sounds of death metal and drunken guests that filtered into the lobby. There was some sort of party going on in the common room.

As they walked to the elevator, Marcus surveyed the room. People milled about a pool table that stood on the far side. Vending machines covered much of the wall. On the left, chairs and couches formed a circle around a beer-strewn table. The elevator doors opened, and they stepped in.

Before the elevator closed, a pale-faced boy, maybe sixteen years old, thrust his head in front of the doors. He had a silver loop that pierced his nose, and a cigarette dangled from his lips.

They walked down the hall and entered their room. They would share one bunk bed, and after Marcus dropped their bags and looked around, he wanted to take Kia and Ben away because the room had two other bunk beds with wooden lockers tucked beside them, and across from his bed, several anarchist flags and an effigy of the Republican president slumped beneath the opposite bed.

"We might not be staying here," Marcus said, remembering the pale-faced boy from downstairs. Kia hadn't heard. She climbed into the bottom bunk and was feeding Benjamin. Afterwards, she dug into a bag and pulled out a sandwich.

"Any more of those?" Marcus said. His mother had made a dozen of them, and her fingerprints still marked the white bread.

Maybe he ought to call Leroy, but it was getting late, nearly midnight, and Kia wanted to sleep. He was also tired.

"Kia," he said, after he checked the strength of the wooden guardrail on the upper-bunk, "why don't you and Ben stay in the upper-bunk until we see these roommates.

I'll sleep down here." He said it while studying the effigy beneath the bunk across from him. The painter had colored the effigy's eyes with thickly laid red acrylic.

After midnight, three young men shuffled into the room. Two of them were laughing, but one of them, the largest (his boots clomping heavily on the floor, a sturdy hipped young man) snapped at them to shut up.

"We've got roommates," he hissed and biffed someone's head.

Marcus lay on top of his covers, fully dressed, his boots still laced up.

The three young men (the sturdy legged one, a tall skinny one with long hair, and another smallish guy) peeled off their black clothes, their bodies all at once pale.

In the morning, one straggler, the smallish one with the nose ring, sprawled on the bed, complaining he was sick. He couldn't have weighed more than a hundred pounds. His friends cursed him when he refused to wake, the sturdy one tugging at the skinny guy's nose ring. When that hadn't worked, he braced his hands on the top of the upper-bunk's railing and jutted his boot into the boy's ribs.

Marcus sat up and scooted back in the lower bunk. While the assailed young man guarded himself, the beefy one thrust his boot into his chest and groin, each kick smacking into his face or chest or legs.

Benjamin Marco coughed, upset, and let out a piercing cry. Blood oozed from the beaten boy's mouth, and the others walked, red-faced and embarrassed like children, towards the door, with the effigy hanged on a pole over the tall one's shoulder.

"Sorry for the disturbance," the sturdy-legged boy said and tipped an imaginary hat.

After they'd left, the boy tore off his t-shirt and pressed it over his face. He lay that way, completely still, for a minute. Marcus leaned forward.

"Hey," Marcus whispered, "you all right?"

Marcus thought the young man would speak. His body quivered, and Benjamin Marco suddenly silenced. Then the young man made a sound. It was a pitiful, stretched out groan Marcus could feel in his own throat.

The young man paused to suck in air, then made the sound again, louder and more hoarsely. He lay in a fetal position in the middle of the mattress, the t-shirt hiding his eyes and nose. Thin blood smeared his teeth, and soon sobs filled the space between his moaning.

Marcus stepped from the bed and turned. Kia held Benjamin to her chest and had pushed herself into the corner against the wall. She had a hand clamped over her mouth. Tears filled her eyes. Her expression asked Marcus to do something.

Marcus bent towards the young man in the bottom bunk. "Hey, buddy," he said, "hey." He stood up and turned towards Kia. "Should we call the police?"

"No!" It was the young man.

"Why not?" Boot marks reddened over the boy's body.

"He's my brother!"

They left the hostel, the beaten boy asleep in the bottom bunk, and waited in the front lobby. When Marcus had called for Leroy, Nurse Sheila had answered. Members of the organization were staying on the ground floor. Kia and Ben Marco, they'd decided, would go with Sheila and Squirrel to the forum. Marcus, after getting his hair cut, would meet them there.

Downstairs in the lobby, Sheila leaned against a support beam. She wore chic sunglasses and had bundled her locks in bristly sticks behind her head. Behind her, the chunks of ice that had formed along the gutters dripped down in steady streams.

"You're going to speak today," Sheila said.

Marcus nodded, then wagged a finger at Sheila and Kia. "You two be good till then."

Sheila pursed her lips. "Not walking with a cane no more?"

Marcus blushed. "Ask my wife," he said, and as the two women departed towards the rooms, Marcus flung open the main doors and scooped together a slushy snowball. He lobbed it across the lobby, and it crumbled against Sheila's shoulder.

Sheila screamed, scandalized, and Marcus retreated through the melting snow.

CHAPTER 10

The church Marcus would speak in was in Chinatown. Marcus took the metro and found the barbershop a block away. He relaxed in the barber chair and laid his head back. A woman's fingers scrubbed his head in the sink. Water from the faucet splashed down the drain. The shampoo smelled of pine.

The barber murmured as she rinsed his head. Marcus closed his eyelids, and when he opened them, the drying towel flashed over his head. It looked like a tumbling leaf.

After the cut, he walked along the sidewalk. Houses crowded together, brightly colored solid blue, green, and yellow. The houses sharpened at their tops with gothic roofs. Voices jeered all around him, but, for the moment, the street looked empty of demonstrators. Crowds somewhere beyond shouted. The voices crested when he passed alleyways. Other walkers on the sidewalk gripped coats tighter around their necks and bent forward in the cold, no signs of worry on their faces. He walked on.

Down the street, the source of the shouting at last appeared. In the middle of the intersection, young men wearing masks and dressed entirely in black used sticks to swat an effigy of the newly reelected president. The effigy hung from an electrical line and dangled over the crossroads. The men regrouped on one corner and milled around, the big guy from the hostel taunting passing cars.

Marcus climbed up a slope of snowy grass and came to a park. The snow was melting. He trudged through the slush until he came to a path that led to the church. From the park, the street with tall, narrow Victorian houses resembled a street of watching faces. The doors were mouths that intoned. He climbed up cement steps and walked into the vestibule.

Kia was waiting just inside, shadows on the walls. Marcus kissed her, caressed his son's forehead, and turned downstairs to speak.

About the Author

Justin Nicholes, from Ashtabula County, Ohio, has appeared in American Poets Abroad, Luna Negra, and Karamu. He is on the editorial board of Our Stories literary journal and has an MFA from Wichita State. He is currently teaching writing in Xinzheng City, in the Henan province of China. He will soon be returning to the United States to focus on completing his next novel.

CLICK
a novel by Kristopher Young

Official Book Club selection on Chuck Palahniuk's The Cult!

Official Book Club selection on Oxyfication.net!

"This is a voice that reaches out and goes right for the jugular."

-*Detroit Metro Times*

"...the author has pulled off a rare and amazing literary feat: he has crafted a work that is highly personal and gut–wrenchingly real, yet surreal, dream–like and convincingly fantastic. The novel is both intuitive and masterful in execution, and in this regard it shares more with the spirit of modernist painting than it does with postmodern literature. Young speaks to us in a voice that is authentic and thoroughly lacking in pretension."

-*Jody Franklin, editor, Mungbeing*

"A compelling genre–bending piece of fiction with a great hook. CLICK embodies the grit–lit of the streets, an element of science fiction and a smattering of a thriller, a picture of a man at war with the world and with himself, right until the final pages when the last click comes 'harsh and loud and true.'"

-*Susan Tomaselli, editor, Dogmatika*

CLICK'S HERO IS experiencing glitches in the universe. He may have tapped into a strange ability which gives him control over the world around him. Or, there's the disturbing possibility that he's a case study in paranoid schizophrenia. After all, they might be after him. He's falling apart—and to make matters worse, his girlfriend may just be crazier than he is. Forced to face his fears and come to terms with his own flawed nature, he must discover what it means to truly evolve.

ISBN 0-9776051-0-8

THE GOLDEN CALF
a novel by Henry Baum

"This pacy, tightly written novel is like 'Taxi Driver' meets Charles Bukowski's *Factotum*."
-*Uncut*

"An amusing, persuasive insight into obsession, stalking and the disintegration of sanity. Highly recommended to anyone with a bitter hatred of Tom Cruise and Hollywood stars in general."
-*Butterfly*

"A marvel of pace and comic timing.... Much of Baum's narrative bears a similarity to *Dostoevsky's Notes from the Underground*."
-*Daily Telegraph*

"With a superb narrative control, Baum paints a portrait of male dysfunction set to explode."
-*The List*

"Ray is nearly as good a portrait of post-collegiate angst as has been painted so far."
-*New York Press*

"Explores the hazy junction where the teeth of the daily grind sink into the day-dreamt certainties of life's true bell-head sounds."
-*Lee Ranaldo, member of Sonic Youth*

RAY TOMPKINS IS the kind of person you never get to know. He's the security guard, the factory worker, the man working the midnight shift. Nobody really understands Ray - not his coworkers, not his family, and certainly not the women in his life. There is a rage building inside Ray Tompkins and Los Angeles is the fuel - the sick obsession with celebrity mixed with the vacuousness of everyday life. Against this backdrop, Ray Tompkins finds a way to vent his anger. He, too, will be known...

ISBN 0-9776051-5-9

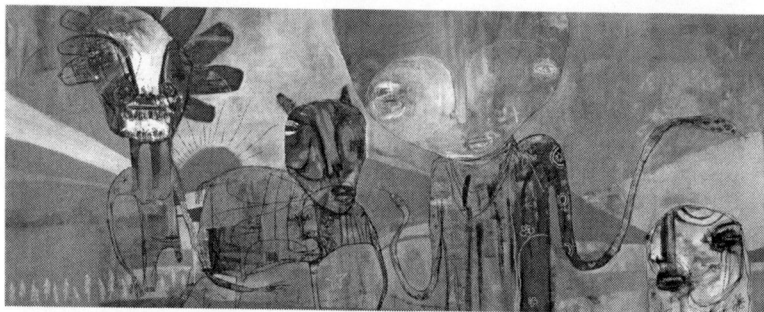

TRUTH WILL MEASURE
the art of Jesse Reno

OVER 100 FULL-COLOR WORKS from one of today's most prolific outsider artists, Jesse Reno. Self-taught, Reno's distinctive style has emerged through sheer creative will. Reaching deep into his subconscious and the wisdom of our ancestors, Reno has created a mythology that permeates his work, both defining and defying the lasting conflict between man and nature. Inspired by indigenous, primitive, and shamanic painters, Reno is at once artist and story-teller, speaking a truth that makes viewing his work not just an experience, but a journey.

"The innate beauty of Reno's engaging, many-layered paintings invites the viewer into the artist's complex personal mythology... In assimilating the message that individuals have the power to change for the better, the viewer understands that Reno, beyond being an artist, is able to assume the role of contemporary shaman—accessing totemic symbols for the purpose of restoring equilibrium between human beings and the environment..."

-BLK/MRKT GALLERY, Los Angeles, California

ISBN 0-9776051-3-2

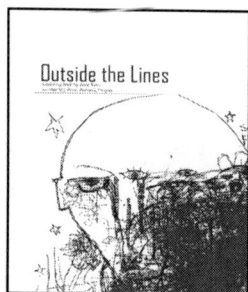

Outside the Lines

OUTSIDE THE LINES
a coloring book
by Jesse Reno

ISBN 0-9776051-1-6

Printed in the United States
202672BV00001B/55-156/P